FUDGE

An oil man's tale

Stephen Kendall

Grosvenor House
Publishing Limited

This book is published by
Grosvenor House Publishing Ltd
Link House
140 The Broadway, Tolworth, Surrey, KT6 7HT.
www.grosvenorhousepublishing.co.uk

This book is a work of fiction. Any resemblance to
people or events, past or present, is purely coincidental.

A CIP record for this book
is available from the British Library

Paperback ISBN 978-1-83615-374-0
eBook ISBN 978-1-83615-375-7

Foreskin... sorry, Foreword

Steve Kendall was raised in the South East London suburbs and was the product of a sad comprehensive education. About the only pupils of distinction to hail from Sedgehill Secondary Modern were Status Quo, the rock band. They are still waiting for their first Prime Minister. (I guess if John Major can make it, we must all be in with a shout!) On recent form, he or she just might make a go of it, as bullying, deceit, and flagrant bullshitting were a pre-requisite for survival in such an environment. It's my understanding that M&S do a nice Teflon overcoat so nothing will stick. The thought of a £7million payday for your memoirs and the lecture circuit, and of course your entry into the happy world of shares in companies that peddle death, are certainly an incentive for the mostly ambitious of individual.

On leaving Sedgehill Secondary Modern with a Double First in Ducking and Diving and Bobbing and Weaving (University Challenge would not entertain them, as they thought it grossly unfair to their opponents), and with a flood of offers ranging from Oxbridge, Sandhurst, The City, Lloyds, and Whitehall, Steve Kendall told them all to "Go forth and multiply". And with the certain knowledge that good old Blighty would always be there for him wherever he may roam, he set out to find himself in a variety of jobs, which took him to the nether reaches of the planet. Some were pleasant places, most were dire.

Steve Kendall resides in New Zealand with his first and only wife and three kids.

The Wedding

Fudge, aka Peter Fudge, often wondered how he found himself in his present situation. He had said to himself that if he had handled situations differently, maybe a little less belligerent, a little more deviously, and maybe not so in-your-face, he would not be standing in this overpowering heat saturated with humidity and faint with exertion.

He guessed it started many years before, with a wedding of a friend of his from the same council estate in S.E. London. All had gone reasonably well throughout the ceremony, and both sides of the family were now crammed into a tiny two-bed, mid-terraced house for the reception. Her lot were on one side of what passed as a living room and also scattered around the kitchen; his lot made up the rest of the limited space.

Trouble started when it came to the cutting of the cake. The photographer had been summonsed, and everyone gathered around for the ritual of him and her holding the same knife as it delicately penetrated the outer layer of the cake. Only problem was, somebody had got there first – and a huge wedge of cake was missing. The bride broke down in tears, and a cry went up, "Who's the asshole who's done this?"

On surveying the living room, draped across the settee lay JC (Jonny Carmann), with a pint of bitter in one hand and what remained of the wedge of cake in the other. Around his mouth could be seen specks of marzipan, and scattered down the front of his shirt were crumbs and currants.

"Uncouth pig" came a lilting cry from a man from the valleys, looking resplendent in his Marks & Spencer grey flannels and Harris tweed jacket, courtesy of the Pontypridd Heart Foundation shop.

But what really set the whole thing off was the groom breaking into an almost uncontrollable fit of laughter, instead of supporting his new beloved. Very quickly the whole affair started to take on ugly undertones. Her lot had travelled up from Wales in number. Ronnie, the groom, was orphaned, so his only family consisted of a few ex-Royal Navy mates and street kids, including Fudge, and they were vastly outnumbered.

Fortunately, what remained of the reception was saved by the vicar who had performed the wedding ceremony. With charm and diplomacy, he managed to defuse the situation.

That night, as Fudge lay in bed, he had made a vow to himself: *I'll get out of this shithole whatever it takes.* He had watched numerous boys from the estate get married at seventeen to the girl from around the corner. Their dad had gone down the council office and somehow wangled a council house for them to live in, and what remained of their lives – after knocking out three kids by their twenty-first birthday – was the local working man's club and the betting shop.

Salvation had come in an advertisement Fudge spotted in a discarded *Daily Telegraph* whilst on his way to work at the biscuit factory. It only consisted of three lines in the Engineering column, and a telephone number. During the morning break, Fudge called the number, and a pleasant French lady noted his work experience and told him to be at a certain Heathrow Airport hotel on the Saturday morning to meet up with Mr. Alain Dumerre.

Fudge, all 6feet 2ins of him, with good looks and a fine physique, was at the appointed location with thirty minutes to spare. Around fifteen other young hopefuls were also in attendance. Fudge and all the rest sat through various technical tests explaining the difference between petrol and diesel engines – all very basic stuff to the technically gifted Fudge. After a one-hour lunch, during which time Fudge assumed the papers had been marked, the polite French lady called in several of the candidates. It did not take much working out: either they were selected leaving Fudge and co on their way home, or vice versa.

The assembled group began to feel a little more optimistic as time passed, as they reckoned if they were out, they probably would have been given their travel expenses by now and released. The French lady appeared once more and called a name, and a young man sprang to his feet and went into a room. After about twenty minutes, another hopeful was called. Fudge was third in line.

He shook hands firmly with Dumerre and waited to be asked to be seated. Dumerre's English was perfect, and he conveyed to Fudge that his results, although not the best, were certainly adequate for the work about to be offered. If Fudge was interested, he would be on his way to Paris for eight weeks' training in oilfield technology and then be assigned to a Middle Eastern base, working a six-on four-off regime for what Fudge considered to be good money. It was obvious that if a company were going to all the expense of training people and shipping them to various parts of the world, the work would be extremely demanding, but this was compensated by salary.

Fudge was aware of the high failure rate in the oil industry, but this was his release from what he considered to be the prison of council estate life. So, the following Monday, he handed in his notice and dispatched his passport to the required office.

Prior to his departure to Paris, Fudge had a gathering of what remained of his friends in their local for a farewell drink. The general feeling amongst this motley gang was "Fudge won't last five minutes in that shithole".

The scheduled training was abruptly cut short for Fudge in Gay Paris, though, as the overly efficient lady in the London company office had pre-empted his movements and had already arranged a Saudi visa. It became apparent to Fudge very early on that in this business "flexibility of movement was a necessity".

The harsh environment of the Saudi desert was in stark contrast to the mean streets of South East London. With searing midday heat to the extreme chill of night, Fudge felt an affinity with the place. In quiet periods, he would often drive off into the desert in the company 4x4, over sand dunes as big as apartment blocks. Then he would switch off the engine and spend hours surveying the endless desert, his only company being his transistor radio as he tuned into the BBC for the football to see how his beloved Arsenal was doing, or to listen to John Peel. Most of his music was crap, but he liked Peel's patter, and it gave him a sense of home.

He marvelled at how wildlife could survive such a hostile environment. On many an occasion he worked a remote location, and he would encounter a Bedouin camp. Without fail, he would stop and say "Hello". He often asked himself how a family could eke out a life and survive there, and he never failed to be moved by the Bedouin generosity. Neither party understood one word the other was saying, but sincere warmth passed between them with a handshake and the ceremonial cup of tea.

Fudge spent four years in various Middle East locations, and in that time met a cross-section of Arab society, from the humble Bedouin on the one hand to the powerful Emirs who became the compulsory Arab partners for the big multinationals. Regardless of their position, generosity seemed to be the common thread. Fudge was to later reflect on how that was to all change, and on his return to the Middle East some years later, he was treated with suspicion and distaste.

Even though Fudge worked in an all-male environment, deep down he was a very sensitive man who loathed cruelty to animals and could not condone violence in any shape or form. This flew in the face of his workplace, where redneck Americans were dominant, hunting magazines were strewn across the mess room tables, and conversations were about wars and killing.

With so much time spent in the desert, his body was naturally tanned in a way no sunbed could achieve, and the work being so physical meant he was in top condition. In the London clubs he frequented, the young ladies seemed attracted to his vulnerabilities, and when the veneer was stripped away from the strutting peacocks who also did the circuit, Fudge never wanted for female company.

During his time in the Middle East, Fudge had the savvy to piss only half his money away on fast cars and fast women; the other half he invested in a couple of apartments – one of which he called home. To most of his neighbours' consternation, his apartment was little more than a bedding ground for the procession of ladies that passed through.

With his looks, physique, and apparel befitting a man doing OK for himself, Fudge stood out from the crowd. On one occasion he invited a lady home for dinner and rattled the pots and pans and put the wine on ice. As they sat on the settee, for some unknown reason Fudge turned on the television and he saw a very disturbing report from the Middle East. An Arab man was lying in the street trying to protect his son, as they had somehow become caught up in crossfire between rioters and the might of the Israeli war machine. A tear rolled down Fudge's cheek as he watched this solitary man pitted against Abram tanks, F14s, and American-made machine guns in the futile attempt of trying to save his son. Any attempt at lovemaking that night was lost as they lay in bed, yet instead of being offended and storming out of the apartment, the young lady consoled him in such a caring and loving way that it restored his faith in the human race.

His beliefs that the Arabs were getting a raw deal in the Middle East were further strengthened when a certain high-ranking British M.P., who had travelled to the Middle East and had the balls to say it was an affront to humanity the way these people were being treated by the Israelis, was in turn set up by certain infamous journalist with a hidden agenda. The journalist knew of the M.P.'s dalliance with a certain lady who had a predilection for football outfits.

And so Fudge's sojourn in the Middle East ended, and now he stood on what passed for a drill ship in the Bay of Bengal, contemplating how he was going to endure the next six weeks eating nothing but omelettes and cornflakes. The occasional curry sat OK with Fudge, but three times a day would put a strain on his stomach, and in particular his bowels. Past experience had told him that too much crapping, too much heat, too much sweating, and too much residue from un-rinsed-out, cheap washing powder in your underpants, would leave you with a fearful dhobi breakout and a crippling red rash either side of your nuts that would render you walking like a ninety-five-year-old.

The Anglo Yank

One of Fudge's crew was another Brit whose dad had got webbed up with an American girl many years before. As a result of living many years in oil-related cities in the southern states of American, he had developed a real Southern drawl. Over many conversations at the coffee table and many cigarettes, Fudge discovered that Brett had a brother back in the U.K.

Fudge assumed the brother must have stayed behind with their mum when hubby took off for what he thought would be greener pastures over the other side of the pond. It transpired that Brett, on his days off, was going back to the U.K. to attend his brother's wedding.

"A big affair?" asked Fudge.

"Big affair would be an understatement," replied Brett. "My brother is a fiercely ambitious man who's got his eyes firmly fixed at the top. He's marrying a Jewish girl whose father owns a big operation, which by all accounts supplies just about every new house build in the U.K. with kitchen equipment."

"He sounds serious about this."

"Serious enough to have the snip and immerse himself in Judaism. My brother was born with the brains, got a scholarship to a top grammar school, went to uni and then into the city to work for a merchant bank. Sadly, all I got was the brawn."

Fudge pondered how his life had run parallel to Brett's. He, too, had a brother who had won a scholarship to the local grammar. But in his case, he loathed with a passion the upper middle-class children that attended the same school. He was vastly superior in intelligence, made very little attempt at his studies – much to the frustration of his masters – but had the ability when it mattered to pass exams. He could have gone onto a good uni, but instead dropped out, met a girl, they had a baby and now lived in a squat in Deptford.

One ciggy coffee break, Fudge told Brett, "If my brother had been born in Germany at the time of the Baader-Meinhof gang, he would have shown the same enthusiasm to anarchy as your brother shows toward ambition. Either way, they are probably both intolerable, insufferable prats."

The weeks passed by and the friendship between Fudge and Brett grew accordingly. In the oilfield business, close proximity to fellow working men and the sheer difficulty of the work in such a harsh environment meant an inevitable clash of personalities. So, it was a relief to come up against somebody who was of similar nature, had a good sense of humour, and was not trying to get somewhere in life at the expense of somebody else. Fudge had had many a run-in with men who were supposedly work colleagues, but the minute they were back in town began bad mouthing him.

And he knew he would never get on the management ladder, as he didn't have the required slyness to make it. He could count on one hand the number of decent managers he had worked under; men who were good to their word, tried to play fair, and treated their boys with respect. Sadly, they invariably only made the first rung of the ladder. The men who really made it were always out of the same mould – calculating, devious, with a memory that was selective, and with absolutely no conscious or decency.

Steve Frankman was the best example that came to Fudge's mind. He and Fudge had nearly come to blows on more than one occasion, and Frankman had done his level best to get Fudge the bullet. But higher management knew Fudge's value and had none of it.

Fudge had seen hard men virtually reduced to tears where they had been promised the world while in reality they were being used and abused. Sadly for these men, their managers knew of their circumstances. Invariably, they were on their second or third marriage, children were involved, mortgages, vehicles, and all the accoutrements of the supposed good life which made them vulnerable and at the mercy of their managers. So, they were in no position to tell them to "stick it where the sun don't shine". Fudge, though, was different. With only the proverbial "dick to keep", they had no hold over him. He knew it, management knew it, and management knew he knew it, so they tended to stay away and leave him to do what he was paid for – work.

Living in London, a totally non-oil field city, he was never privy to any of the cushy numbers that occasionally came along, and never on the inside for the latest gossip or scandal. But this suited Fudge. When work was over, all he wanted to do was go home and relax, meet up with his circle of friends, play golf, watch football, and do the club circuit. He always wanted to head straight home from some far-off location, whereas most of the married men would stay over in Bangkok or similar seedy locations for a couple of days of R&R before dutifully going home to the wifey and kids. Fudge loathed with a passion the oilfield towns with their oilfield mentality, where talk was only oilfield, and men were shagging their best mate's oilfield wife.

When the job in India came to an end, Fudge invited Brett back to his apartment to stay over, relax, have a couple of nights out, let him get in contact with his brother, and just generally chill out.

"You really have got it made here," said Brett. "Nice top floor apartment, nice car outside the door. You really don't want for anything."

"Life is not bad at the moment," conceded Fudge.

"The only thing I've noticed missing since I've been here is a woman," Brett commented. "Am I missing something?"

"There have been a couple of serious relationships, but as you are well aware, oilfield and relationships don't go together."

"Why don't you get out while you still have time?" Brett queried.

"Find me a job that pays similar money, gives me nearly half a year off, and I'm yours," came back Fudge.

"Oilfield can put a strain on a relationship. I saw it with my own mum and dad, and there is no doubt once you are in, it's a bitch getting out."

Fudge asked, "Surely your brother must be well connected in the city. Can't he do something for you?"

"My brother is way, way above being able to do something like that," Brett told him. "He really is mixing it with the big boys in the city. I'd be an embarrassment to him. I'll stay where I am."

"Have you made contact with him since you have been in London?" asked Fudge.

"Sure have. Seems he is having a stag night in some club in town. Oh, and by the way, you have been invited."

The Brother

Fudge and Brett took a taxi into town and found themselves in a bar where invitation-only got you through the door. Brett and his brother Terry took each other in an embrace, then Fudge was duly introduced. Fudge was immediately struck by Terry's presence – the firm handshake and those searching piercing blue eyes. This was one man you crossed at your peril.

Brett and Fudge were introduced to various luminaries and company hangers-on, and it was obvious from the off that they were only being tolerated because Brett was family. This was an exclusive world, and entry was purely by connection, the old school tie, or sheer determination by an individual who would have to endure innuendo, sarcasm, and hostility. Terry was such an individual.

Before long, Brett and Fudge were left to themselves, discarded almost, and so they started to hit the source. Occasionally, a young lady looking devastatingly overdressed would pass pleasantries and then move on when it became obvious to her that there was nothing in it for her. It became clear to Fudge that this must be Terry's regular watering hole, as he noted the consumption of alcohol that was being devoured yet no money was passing hands. Terry was picking up the tab at the end of the night, so he must be a trusted customer.

As the night progressed, it came home to Fudge how this company were acting so very differently to what he usually encountered. There seemed to be an unusual amount of activity around one particular individual, and when Fudge pointed this out to Terry, he was informed that if a little Charlie would be to his liking, that was your man. Cocaine, though, had never interested Fudge. He'd had a bad experience once with LSD, and now alcohol was his drug of choice.

As the booze and drugs started to have their effects, and more and more cocaine was being consumed, the company seemed to split into its various component parts. Some acted in a spaced-out fashion, some looked morose, and others seemed to become seriously aggressive. Terry was in his element. He was composer, conductor, and lead man in this opera.

Fudge wondered if Terry himself was partaking in the drug binge, or if it was purely for the others while he stayed on the periphery and controlled the show. Brett and Fudge seemed to become the centre of attention. Had the oilfield boys been invited to the show as entertainment? Fudge was the first to note the barbed comments, and at first he ignored them. But as the night went on, so did the ferocity of the sarcasm.

Finally, Fudge had had enough, and he asked no-one in particular, "How does the 'old boy' network work? Playing with each other at prep school, blow jobs at Eton, and then full-scale turd tapping at Oxbridge?"

"Oooh," went the crowd, followed by sniggers.

Fudge had risen to the bait; he'd been reeled in. But as far as he and Brett were concerned, the entertainment was over. When Terry came in from nowhere and took control of the situation, Fudge had to ask himself,

How far would this man go in the pursuit of getting to the top?

God only knows what time Brett and Fudge got home that morning, but Fudge was awoken by the telephone. Terry's voice was one of somebody who had already showered, been down to the gym, and eaten breakfast; Fudge's was the voice of somebody who had a throat like the bottom of a bird cage.

"Trust you enjoyed your night?"

"Yeah, sure," was about all Fudge could manage. "Hold on a minute and I'll get you Brett."

"That's OK. Just tell Brett not to be late for the ceremony, and should you still be in the country, I'd be happy to see you at the reception; I could do with some troops on my side. You'll understand the ceremony itself is family. It will take place in Chester, and Brett has the details. A hotel has been booked for the weekend, so you don't have to come home straight away. See you there."

Was that a question or a summons? Either way, the telephone call had come to an abrupt halt before Fudge could answer.

The Reception

Fudge and Brett had casually made their way up north in Fudge's Mk 2 Jag and booked into the assigned hotel, which naturally was the best in town. Chester being a very affluent and conservative city, Fudge instinctively knew he would be moving with the serious people. He guessed he must have equipped himself well at the stag night, as he would not be there now if he was a potential embarrassment. Terry most certainly would not tolerate that.

The reception itself was in a ballroom, the likes of which Fudge had never seen before. Flower arrangements were in abundance, and however the Jewish community conduct their wedding ceremonies, those formalities were soon over and done with. A band – or would it best be described as a mini orchestra? – had set up shop and were playing introductory music as the guests slowly arrived and were introduced to the families of the newly married couple.

Upon Fudge's entry, he clapped eyes on Brett and made his way over. His friend had obviously dispensed with the wedding plumage and changed into a casual suit. Fudge looked pretty good in his apparel, but he was too painfully aware that in this gathering he came up woefully short. The designer clothes both the men and women were wearing most certainly were not out of Top Shop.

Terry came over to both Fudge and Brett, and it was apparent he was in a different frame of mind to the stag night. Fudge guessed there would be no Charlie at this bash. "Help yourselves to whatever you would like," he told them. "I would suggest you go a little easy to begin with, but I can assure you by the time this night is over with, you will know you have been to a celebration."

As the night progressed, so did the tempo of the occasion. Fudge was introduced to the bride by Terry, and she was a devastatingly good-looking woman. He also exchanged pleasantries with the bride's mother and was surprised at the warmth she showed him.

As was sometimes his wont, Fudge took time out on his own and walked into the beautiful hotel gardens. There, he reflected on this occasion and the last wedding he had attended in South East London with the hacked-up wedding cake and the very-near fight. He couldn't help wondering where that particular bride and groom were at this moment. Were they still together? Were there kids involved? And how could the divide between then and now be so vast?

After a short while, he made his way back into the ballroom, ordered a spritzer, and found his eyes transfixed on a young lady who was drifting between guests, holding conversations here and there. This lady had an infectious charm for whoever she conducted a conversation with and easily enjoyed their undivided attention.

"Beautiful, isn't she?"

The comment took Fudge totally by surprise, and he turned to see a diminutive lady looking up at him.

"I'm a people watcher, and I've been watching you watching her. That's Rebecca, and she is the bride's sister. I'm their Aunt Estelle." The diminutive lady offered her hand.

As Fudge took it in his, he couldn't help smile at how delicate and small her hand was.

'Those hands have seen some work in their time, young man, and I do not mean punching a keyboard," she said, making Fudge immediately feel at ease.

Estelle Sayer stood no more than five foot two inches in height. Her hair had been worked on at a salon where only the most talented of colour artists plied their trade, and it was styled in such a way it showed off her beautiful eyes, which sat behind glasses, the frames of which were so fragile. Her pure silk costume was understated – maple leaves entwined with ivy – and shoes from an exclusive boutique. The whole ensemble said one thing: class.

Fudge guessed her origins were Eastern, from her very slightly owlish nose. And he couldn't help wonder how many men this lady had devastated in her youth, how many successful high-profile businessmen she had very nearly led to suicide. He was to find out later that this lady was one of the lucky ones to escape Poland, when most of her family didn't make it. Against the family's wishes, after the war she met and married a soldier who was not part of her religion. But the family gave their blessings and support, along with the financial clout for them to initially start a business stripping down batteries for lead, then onto moving vast amount of various metals on differing markets. Sadly for Estelle, when it was time for her husband to hand the company on, he suffered a massive heart attack and died.

"Aunt Estelle, you really are a minx. I leave you alone for five minutes, and there you are talking to this gorgeous hunk of a man," Rebecca planted an affectionate kiss on

Aunt Estelle's cheek. "I am almost sure I would know you if you were from my side of the family," she said to Fudge, offering her hand. "So I must presume you are with the groom."

"Actually I'm a gate crasher. I work with the groom's brother in the oil industry," was the best a nervous Fudge could come up with.

"One of those Ruffy Tuffy oilmen. I thought they were all rednecks and lowlifes?' queried Rebecca.

'Some of us try to rise above that," he stuttered.

"So, where are we all going regarding oil?" she asked. "Am I going to have to forgo the car and walk?"

"I think we can safely say there's enough oil around for you not to have to do that," replied Fudge. "What is your line of work?"

"I work for a diamond dealer."

"Sounds interesting."

She shrugged. "Spend most of my time in an aeroplane, flying between London, Antwerp, and New York, if you call that interesting."

Aunt Estelle could see she was making up the numbers and diplomatically interjected, "There's Bernard, I've not seen him in years. Must say hello." And she took her leave.

Fudge's natural shyness had fully kicked in, and Rebecca sensed this. Here was a lady who had met and moved with some very influential and powerful people. It was no doubt a prerequisite of her position to put these people at their ease with courtesy, conversation, and charm, and above all a professional understanding of both the client's and her bosses' needs. She stood looking at Fudge, making no effort to continue the conversation.

Fudge needed help. And it came in the ungainly shape of Maurice Tolson. "Rebecca, I'm still waiting for that dance that you promised me."

"Just be a little more patient, Maurice. I'll see you very shortly. We're just putting the world to rights regarding the oil crisis." Rebecca's eyes never left Fudge's as she spoke, and Maurice walked away deflated.

"Friend of yours?" asked Fudge.

"He's been trying to get inside my underpants since God knows when," replied Rebecca.

"Trust he's not succeeded?" came back Fudge.

"He's got more chance of finding a foreskin in Tel Aviv than doing that," she told him, all the time continuing with that look.

"Rebecca," he began, "I think you can see I'm not very good at this chatting up business."

"Really? I think you are using your shyness to your advantage, and you know what, it's working. Look, I have to do the rounds, dutiful sister and all that, but I will see you before the night is out."

Rebecca took her leave and made for Marice Tolson, whose face lit up when she took his hand and led him to the dance floor. It was Fudge's turn to look at Rebecca now, but she gave no indication that she was aware of his interest, although deep down he knew she was adoring ever second of his attention.

As if on cue, Terry appeared from nowhere. "See you've made an impact on Rebecca."

"Terry, is there anything you don't miss?" asked Fudge.

Terry awarded himself a smile. "Life's a game, Fudge. I'm convinced you come on this planet with a hand of cards – four to be precise. First card – your stature, i.e.

build, looks; second card – intelligence and how it's used; third card – health and how it's used; and fourth, and by no means the least important – luck. Right place, right time. You didn't come out too badly, Fudge my boy. I'd say a Queen, two Jacks, and a ten. The game of life, of course, is how you play those cards."

"What were you dealt, Terry?" asked Fudge.

"Come, come, Fudge. You never tell anybody what you're holding," replied Terry with a knowing wink. "Wouldn't be a game if I told you that, would it?" Terry leaned back against the bar with a smirk on his face that said he was holding all the aces.

"So, Terry, as a man who's been there and done that, what advice would you give?"

"I really don't think you need any advice, Fudge. I think you are managing very well on your own." "That's disappointing, Terry. I'm sure in your position as a banker you have to continually dispense advice to keep those obscene profits rolling through the door."

"Sarcasm, Fudge, is not only a no-no; it's the first sign you are on the ropes and are about to go down."

"Sadly, Terry, as a product of a very poor secondary modern education, it's probably the only tool I have. Talking of tools, I must go and have a piss."

"Don't be crude, Fudge." As Fudge turned to make for the toilet, Terry's parting shot was, "Keep those cards close to your chest."

Terry was right regarding the celebration. It was gone midnight, and the party was in full swing. The band had packed up but had been invited to stay on to enjoy the disco if they wished. Rebecca was engrossed in a conversation with the trumpet player whilst they danced. It was obvious he was giving it his best to impress her, and Fudge guessed telephone numbers would be exchanged before the night was out. He was only too aware how many young men, all suitors, were no doubt watching Rebecca. She would be the big prize, with the field all to herself, now that her sister was married. Was the trumpet player going to be another conquest? Another bit of rough before her marriage to a merchant banker or company CEO?

As he stood there, the bride's mother came over and asked, 'What's a good-looking young man like you doing standing there looking sorry for himself? Come, let's have a dance."

Being too polite to refuse, Fudge made his way onto the dance floor. Knowing he had two left feet and was no Fred Astaire, nevertheless he did the best he could. One dance led to another, then another. And whether it was the alcohol or just the company, Fudge began to relax and unwind, which was reflected in his dancing. Catching the disco beat can be intoxicating, and as the perspiration started, so the jacket was dispensed with. Next, the tie disappeared, and the shirt buttons started to come undone.

Mrs Fisher indicated that she had had enough and took her leave, but she insisted Fudge continue. Knowing that eyes were watching his every move, Fudge moved to the beat and heard a voice above the music. "Pretty nifty movement there."

Fudge turned to find Rebecca moving to the rhythm of the disco beat and not a trumpet player in sight.

"Now don't give me all that shy crap," she scolded. "You know you are the best thing here. Take a look around you. You can have any available girl that's here."

"You're embarrassing me."

"Of course I am, and enjoying every second of it."

Fudge moved off the dance floor, hoping Rebecca would follow. Needing a thirst-quenching drink, he headed to the bar and ordered a lime and soda mix. When he turned back, Rebecca stood, still looking, still saying nothing.

"I guess you get asked this all the time," he told her, "and if you do not feel comfortable, I'd rather you say than leave me on a piece of string. But I'd like to see you again for dinner or a movie or something."

Rebecca gave out a loud and instantaneous laugh. "I thought you were never going to ask. Look, we are having an afternoon get-together at our place in Tuppington, and I'll see you there tomorrow. I guess you are a couple, so bring Brett, wherever he is, with you."

Fudge had not noticed the absence of Brett, but he was nowhere to be seen.

"I guess your partner in crime is upstairs humping away. I did notice a few girls early on gagging for it, and he's up there or up somewhere else, duly obliging," she told Fudge.

Was Rebecca trying to be one of the boys with these remarks? he wondered. *Did it all change when confronting a high roller? Did she become prim and proper?*

"That would be nice," he responded, referring to the afternoon invitation.

"I have to start saying goodnight to the guests," she said. "See Terry later, or give him a call in the morning for the address in Tuppington. See you there."

Fudge went to bed that night feeling pretty pleased with himself. He would like to have had company, but you can't have it all.

Next morning, he made his way down for breakfast and noticed all the couples and elderly people were already nearly finished. As he sat down, a waiter made his way over to ask if he wanted tea or coffee.

"Coffee, please."

The waiter explained that there was a buffet at the counter, but Fudge replied that he was fine with just coffee.

Waiters, buffet; he couldn't help but smile to himself. On North Sea oil rigs, it was every man for himself; if you didn't get off your arse, you didn't get fed, simple as that. He finished his coffee and several glasses of water to re-hydrate himself then set off to find Brett.

On knocking on Brett's bedroom door, a voice could barely be heard saying, "Fuck off." Fudge continued with the knocking, and he could hear frantic movements from the other side of the door. Suddenly a key could be heard turning, the door opened, and two young ladies who must have been gagging for it emerged, giggled, then disappeared down the corridor.

When Fudge entered, the bedroom looked like something out of Bosnia. "Good night?" he asked.

Brett, still half comatose, looked up wearily. "The next-door neighbours are either very understanding or had a glass against the wall. Those bitches were wild."

Fudge laughed. "OK, Brett, have a shit and a shave. We've been invited to a bash out in Tuppington, wherever that is."

"I'll pass," came back Brett,

"Don't think so, Brett. This is family, and your presence is expected."

"For fuck's sake," he moaned, "can't a man have a bit of peace around here?"

"Brett, we are pissing with the big dogs here. If you don't want to do it for yourself, then do it for me."

The comment brought Brett to life. "Do it for you? What's going down here?" he asked. "You devious bastard, you're pulling a number with Rebecca, aren't you?"

Fudge did not answer but went into the shower, turned it on, came back, and pulled the sheets off Brett, then left the room. Master of ceremonies extraordinaire Terry had left details of how to get to Tuppington and the address. The first thing that struck Fudge regarding the address was the lack of a number; it was just Melrose Hall.

Fudge and Brett fired up the Mk 2 and proceeded out to Tuppington. "Who were the girls?" asked Fudge.

His friend shrugged. "No idea. Just hope they are not where we are going."

Fudge found Tuppington, and he did not have to ask for directions to Melrose Hall; all he had to do was follow the procession of expensive cars that were all going in one direction. At the Gatehouse, an elderly man approached Fudge's car with a clipboard and asked for a name. Fudge replied, his name was duly ticked off, and he was waved through.

"Wonder what the old boy would do if half a dozen Millwall fans pitched up and wanted entry?" Brett asked.

The answer was there in front of them. A further security gate was in place, only this time it was manned by what Fudge guessed were ex-military policemen. Fudge wondered how many men they could muster at a push – enough to deal with half a dozen football fans, no doubt.

Fudge proceeded on up a pathway lined either side by immaculately trimmed poplar trees, spaced evenly apart to the centimetre. The sound of pea shingle could be heard crunching as it took the weight of the heavy 1960 car.

"Trust your oil seals are good. Would imagine Dad's going to get pretty pissed if you leave a gallon and a half of Castrol on his pathway,' quipped Brett.

The Jag took a final sweep of the pathway and then in front of them stood a magnificent Georgian house. The classical lines and symmetry of the building instantly appealed to Fudge.

"Nice little two up, two down," commented Brett.

A man was giving directions for Fudge to take his place in a line on a lawn. No doubt the retained gardeners were crying seeing their beautiful lawn being used as a parking lot. Circling the house, Fudge and Brett entered a garden on the opposite side of the house to the parking lot. This side of the house held a magnificent Orangery; the panes of glass must be in the hundreds. Lawns extended from the Orangery, sweeping down to the river bank, and a huge marquee had been erected. The ubiquitous Terry greeted them and gave Fudge a look that said "Beware". Music was again being played, only this time in a much more sedate tempo and fashion.

Fudge instinctively looked for the trumpet player.

"He is not here."

"Sorry, what was that?" Fudge looked confused.

"He is not here, the trumpet player. That what's on your mind, isn't it? Seeing if the field is clear."

Fudge turned, and there was that smile, that look. Rebecca was simply but fashionably dressed in an expensive sort of way.

"Mr Travolta, very nice to see you." Mrs Fisher came over and shook hands with Fudge. "Trust I did not wear you out last night on the dance floor?"

Fudge replied that he was still in good shape.

Aunt Estelle was the next to come over. "Young man, how nice to see you. Glad to see you survived the night." Pleasant conversation and small talk continued.

With some time to himself at the buffet counter, it suddenly dawned on Fudge, *Where's the dad in all this. Another people watcher? Or was he up to his neck in deal-making? Or simply stepping back and taking it all in?*

Rebecca was obviously her own woman – successful, independent, headstrong, wilful. *How does a father handle a person like that?* He obviously wants what is best for his girl, and she has probably had a private education, been guided and nurtured. Her father couldn't impose his will, though; not in this day and age. No matter how Victorian he might be in principle, how subservient his wife might have been, 2000-women don't take no shit from anyone – or so the tabloids and women's mags would have us believe.

Brett came over with a look of amusement on his face. "Be ready to leg it."

"What?"

"Be ready to haul arse big time."

"You're not making sense, Brett."

"Those girls last night. Seems one of them is married into this family. She don't look too good today, and I might not be looking too good tomorrow, if you see what I mean."

Rececca came over, "Wasn't very subtle, was it?" She looked at Brett, visibly upset. "You could have at least waited till a more opportune time – let's say, twenty-four hours? But no, you just had to think of yourself first, you selfish bastard."

Terry appeared from nowhere and suggested, nay, ordered Brett to leave. Fudge was about to make his exit with him when Rebecca said, "There's no reason why it should spoil your day. Brett can go to the house and order a taxi."

As Brett slinked off into the house like Tom from a Tom and Jerry cartoon, she added, "What a small-minded arsehole. Anyway, it ends here. Now, where were we last night? I believe you asked me for a date?"

"It looks very much like I'm on my way to Egypt any day now," Fudge replied. "I do not want to rush things, but—"

"Suits me," she replied. "I've got a free week this week. Next week I'm busy like hell."

Fudge asked, "I presume you live in London?"

"Yes. I have an apartment on the Embankment."

"Fine. If I could have your number, I'll get in touch."

Rebecca went off to do the dutiful sister bit, and Mr. Fisher came over and shook Fudge's hand. "I'll show you around the estate. If you wish?' This was an order not a request.

Fudge followed Harry Fisher from the marquee, and they made their way down to the river bank, polite talk accompanying them as they walked. Once bank-side, Harry Fisher turned to look back at the house. Standing only five feet two, he had developed a paunch, which was clearly the result of good living. But what Harry Fisher lacked in height, he more than made up for in presence.

His thick, heavy, horn-rimmed glasses sat on that same owlish nose, out of which piercing blue eyes commanded attention. Fudge wondered how many men and families this man had destroyed in leverage buyouts. Family-owned businesses which had been in the same hands for generations just bought out, asset-stripped, putting dozens – possibly hundreds – of men and women on the dole, selling off the sum of the parts, and making a fortune in the process.

Somehow Fudge could see Terry getting off on that – the kill, the buzz that goes with it. No sympathy for the recipients of the buff envelopes informing them that their loans had been foreclosed, their properties taken as they stood as collateral, only to be sold off at an auction where very few Anglo Saxons would be present. If they were lucky, after the vultures in their high-rise, downtown tower blocks had taken their exorbitant fees, the residents might be left with enough money to buy a cup of tea and a ham sandwich, a lifetime of work in their two hands.

But was Fudge being unfair? This man might very well conduct his business with a degree of ethics. The big-time scandals that were hitting the news headlines every other week were possibly painting every mogul with the same brush. Was Fudge's cynicism taking hold of him? Something inside him said that to be successful in today's world you had to be ruthless; as the saying goes, "Nice guys come second."

"Come, let's walk," requested Harry Fisher.

They moved off away from the big house towards a paddock where several beautiful horses were chewing at grass.

"I understand you work in the oilfield, is that correct?"

Fudge replied in the affirmative.

"Nice to see a young man doing his best and trying to make his way in life. Such a tragedy seeing this youth of today spending inordinate amounts of time and energy bunking the system, getting something for nothing. Eventually it will bring the country down. Already the police can't cope, social services can't cope. God only knows the real cost of keeping it all going. If the public were ever to know the true cost, the billions – yes, billions – of pounds frittered away each month, there would be a riot."

Harry was in full flow now. "I was reading an article about the welfare system in various countries around the world, and it averages out at over 37 per cent of all tax revenues goes into welfare. Such a waste. I feel desperately sorry for the genuine cases, those Army boys coming home messed up and getting no support, where industry has folded and those people are on the scrap heap. And we can't blame the unions anymore; there aren't any, so it has to be down to management and, of course, for the benefit of the politicians, market forces, and movements." There we have it: Harry Fisher, mogul with a conscience, man ahead of his time? Or a disillusioned romantic, and a very wealthy one at that, out of time?

Either way, Fudge had to give this man any benefit of the doubt that he harboured. He had seen his own father, who had worked all his life for one company, treated in a dismal fashion when it was his turn for help. He had visited his father in his council house when social services turned up because the old boy was unable to look after himself anymore.

The social service people were pressuring Fudge to take responsibility for his father. But from the outset,

Fudge had been polite and explained that he worked a six-and-four schedule, so it was just not practicable. This did not, however, appear to satisfy the authorities.

By that stage, Fudge was very pissed off, and a pissed-off Fudge was not a particularly pleasant sight. He asked if they had seen his father's record. When asked what he meant by that, Fudge replied that here was a man who had done his bit for king and country, a hero in shirt sleeves, running round London shutting down gas mains as the doodlebugs were falling and the bombers were dropping their deadly payload, fire lapping at his arse; a man who could count on one hand the number of days he had been off for sickness, and now it was his turn, he was being treated like a leper. In all fairness to social services, they must have gone back to the office smarting and possibly looked up his father's record, as he finished his days in a pleasant rest home on the Essex coast.

"George, the man at the gatehouse, ex-paratrooper dropped into Arnhem, got shot up very badly and had a very bad time at the hands of the Germans. Hard as nails, took it all, everything, the beatings, the torture, came through, then fell apart when his wife died some years ago. Could not even handle going down to the supermarket to get a pint of milk. An acquaintance of mine runs a trust to help these kinds of people. Just couldn't turn him away, and in return I've got a man in a million. Ask Rebecca one day. Somebody was pestering her, George got to hear of it, called in a few of the boys from the regiment, they found him next morning in a park, in agony, arms tied behind his back with the rope thrown over a bough and just enough tension not to dislocate the ball from the shoulder socket."

The words 'ask Rebecca one day' struck Fudge. So Harry Fisher knew Fudge had made a move for his daughter. Was he pleased about this? Would Fudge be tolerated? Fudge was no Terry, no climber, no yes man, no arse wipe – just his own man.

Fudge asked, "What was your history, Mr. Fisher?"

"Born and raised in Poland, forced into the ghetto. My father being a university professor had a little sway and managed to get us children out, but sadly his fate and that of my mother are unclear. The last we heard of them, they were on their way to Treblinka. Never made it. Such a waste, a terrible, terrible waste – doctors, mathematicians, engineers, the best brains in the country. Still, as they say, life must go on.

"Enough of this. It is my daughter's wedding, a time of joy. Seems my new son-in-law's brother went a little over the top with Joy last night."

So, this man has a sense of humour, Fudge thought.

Slowly walking back toward the house, Harry Fisher was asked by Fudge about his future. "As I do not have a son to leave the business to, I will possibly sell up and retire to the Channel Islands," he replied.

So, Terry has been overlooked regarding the family business. Fudge wondered if he was aware of this. He also wondered if Mr Fisher had imparted this piece of knowledge to any of the extended family, as he had no doubt there were close and distant nephews manoeuvring and jockeying for position and being guided by ambitious parents. Must be worth a pretty penny. Not on a public offering, but purely in private hands, this had to be one of the biggest businesses of its kind, supplying housebuilders and DIY stores with kitchens from the budget design right through to the upmarket, top-of-the-range styles.

Fudge offered up, "You have worked hard for it. You deserve your place in the sun."

"Thank you, young man, that's nice to hear."

Fudge and Mr Fisher arrived back at the marquee where they were joined by Rebecca. "What have you two been conspiring about?" she asked.

Rebecca's father replied, "Just small talk, just small talk."

Had Fudge passed the test? Had he gained acceptance? Was he at just first base? Or was he already dead and buried?

Terry swooped down like the proverbial vulture. "How did it go with my father-in-law?"

Fudge noted the emphasis on the 'my'. "Oh, pretty good actually. He really made me feel at ease." Fudge wondered if Terry was ruing inviting him up to be one of his troops. *Did he feel threatened? Was Terry, after all, human and starting to feel there just might be a competitor in the camp? Or was Fudge running away with himself?* After all, they had only just met. If Terry was feeling this insecure after just one weekend, what would it be like if Fudge and Rebecca really hit it off.

He felt like saying to Terry, "Don't sweat, I'll make my own way, thank you very much" but thought better of it.

The rest of the day passed very pleasantly. The day after the night before meant going very easy on the source. One, Fudge was driving; and two, the eyes were watching. There's nothing worse in life than family and money – they just don't mix. Whether it be envy, jealousy, or whatever, nothing can quite destroy a family like money. How many lottery winners usually end up at odds with the family because of somebody's good fortune? And to really put the boot in, here was an outsider, not even of the faith.

Again, Fudge had to check himself not to go over the top. He had to put things into perspective. These people were born into money and a system where education, strong family ties, ambition, and success were a tradition. OK, a madman tried to take it away from them, but when it was ingrained into your society, no amount of persecution can wrench it from you.

Could this be a decent family not driven by greed? Fudge was all too well aware of the Boerskys, the Waksells, the Milkens, the Parnes, the Maxwells, the Lyons – all exceptionally wealthy people mixed up in scandal because they just had to have more. *But was this only linked to one faith?* Ever since his childhood, the Jews had always been denigrated because of their success – most of it borne out of envy – because they tended to be an insular society and kept it within the family. Now there's a contradiction.

"Fudge." Rebecca came toward him with a grin on her face. "Just had a call from the police. That dumb shit Brett had no money with him, but didn't realise it till he got to the hotel. Apparently, he told the taxi driver he was going to his room for the money, and the taxi driver thought he was going to do a runner. It got a bit ugly, and the police were called. Brett is down at the station, waiting for you to pick him up and pay the driver. Now, there's justice for you. Seems they won't press charges."

Fudge found this as amusing as Rebecca, but sadly it meant he would have to take his leave, hurriedly say goodbye and thank you to all, and be on his way. He turned to Rebecca, wishing he could kiss her goodbye, but instead just said, "I'll call, if that's OK with you?"

"Yes, Fudge, that's OK with me." Just as Fudge was turning from Rebecca to go, he looked up to see Terry watching his every move.

Fudge got to the police station, paid an exorbitant taxi fare, and took Brett back to the hotel.

"Guess I've not done much for Anglo-American special relationships, have I?" quipped Brett.

"No, mate, I guess you haven't. When was the last time you saw your brother?"

"Must be the best part of fifteen years."

Fudge shook his head. "Don't count on seeing him in the next fifteen years."

"We were never that close, so I can only imagine he was pressured into having some family representation here," Brett replied with a shrug. "Still, it seems you equipped yourself well."

"Time will tell, Brett, time will tell."

Monday passed into Tuesday and then to Wednesday, and Fudge had heard nothing. He knew any day now he could be mobilized for a job somewhere and was aware of several potential jobs coming up. The fact the company had not asked for his passport for visa processing narrowed it down to a couple of possible locations, with Egypt being the most probable. Fudge didn't mind working the Middle East, and by choice he would rather go there than the bitter cold of the North Sea. The North Sea Tigers were usually out of Aberdeen or Yarmouth.

He mulled over in his mind countless times whether to call Rebecca and try not to seem too gushing, or to sit and wait. Finally, he said to himself, *Screw it! It's shit or bust time.*

The telephone seemed to ring endlessly, then, "Hello." Fudge's heart missed a beat.

"Hope I'm not disturbing you."

"No. I'm surprised it took you so long to call."

"I'm sorry?"

"You did say if it's OK you would call, and I said it's OK. So, I was waiting. Any news as to when you might be going away?"

"No, none." He cleared his throat a little. "I did not want you to feel I was pressuring you."

"No, Fudge, I do not feel pressured."

"If tonight is free, would you like to see a movie, followed by a meal?"

"Fudge, you mean well, but I'm sick and tired of eating out, and I think I've just about seen every movie ever, made courtesy of British Airways. Why don't you make your way up here, bring a pizza and a bottle of white, and let's just sit, listen to some music, and watch a bit of telly?"

"That sounds fine with me." Fudge took an address and directions and was in the Jag and on his way uptown via a pizza house and the wine merchants.

Rebecca's apartment was in a warehouse conversion. A gatekeeper had been informed of his arrival and he was requested to park his car in a visitor's bay. Rebecca's apartment was all that was expected of a high flying lady executive, and entry could only be accessed via video entry phone.

As Fudge entered, Rebecca had just emerged from the shower. She had a bath robe on and a towel wrapped around her wet hair, but she still looked devastating. Rodrigo was playing in the background. Laid on a coffee table made of highly polished Rimu stood two wine glasses and two plates, no knives, no forks. This was a hands-only night.

As usually happens when you are in company you enjoy and feel totally relaxed, the time disappeared and suddenly they realised it was gone one in the morning.

"Don't ask to stay, Fudge. I know I would enjoy it. but I don't think you should."

Fudge had had his fair share of slappers in his time; one-nighters. He was only too thankful he had not picked up something on the way. But this was definitely no slapper.

Rebecca escorted him to the door. "Have to say it was a very pleasant night," she told him. "You will call again?"

They embraced, and when Fudge gave Rebecca a kiss on her lips, she made no move to pull away. Reluctantly, he detached himself and said, "I'll call before the weekend, and that's a promise."

"You do that, Fudge."

Fudge's journey home from London town was the most pleasant drive he had experienced in a long, long time.

Newey

Fudge returned home in the early hours and found there were messages on his answerphone. He instinctively knew there would be one telling him to report for duty. Sure enough, the gruff tones of Phil Newey (his operations manager) told Fudge to be in the office no later than ten the next morning, as he and his crew were booked on the afternoon flight to Cairo then on to the western desert in a taxi.

As always, next morning Fudge was on time and entered Newey's office, carrying his kitbag.

"OK, as you are no doubt aware. I'm tearing my fucking hair out and having a fucking nervous breakdown keeping this piss ant operation going," his boss grumbled. "I've put together a crew. Billy Lush and Nonce are at this very moment sitting in the King George getting blootered. Rumour has it it's Nonce's birthday, and as we are all so well aware Lush doesn't need too many excuses for a drink. I suggest you get down there a bit rapid and get some coffee down their Gregory, otherwise they won't let them on the plane. Next up you've got the Captain."

The Captain had been christened Captain Miserable on a North Sea rig, because he had to be the most miserable bastard on the planet. Lush, in one of his more eloquent moments, had declared, "If the Captain

38

washed up on a desert island with Jordan, he'd still be fucking pissed about something."

Fudge was about to protest, but Newey got in first. "I've heard it all before. Lush is a fucking good hand when he's off the piss, and it's your job to keep him off the piss. As for Nonce, keep him out of the way. As long as he's on the service ticket, we make money, you get paid, and everybody is happy. On the good side, I've managed to get you the Furno, Sweep Meacham, and some boy named George who's out of the Aberdeen pool. Lush has worked with him before and says he's alright. He's as green as grass but he's willing. You'll meet at the airport."

Fudge was OK with the Lush; off the piss, he was a good hand. As for Nonce, warning signs flashed in front of him. Fudge thought him a devious bastard, who acted the Nonce as it kept away from any kind of responsibility on the job. Away from the job, Nonce was up the front for any kind of freebie, whether it be a meal, drink, or complimentary handouts supervisors took with them to give to the boys on the oil rig who helped out on the crane or made up the endless pipe required to carry out a well test. Fudge was convinced Nonce was a grass, because when a job was over and they returned home, he seemed to spend an inordinate amount of time in the office.

Furno was a good hand if the mood suited him. In the same way as furnace explodes molten metal, Furno would explode in a similar fashion if rubbed up the wrong way. Sweep Meacham was what Fudge called "a blinding geezer". He was known as Sweep, because rumour had it he was knocked up in a broom cupboard down The Kings Head in Bermondsey.

By all accounts, his mum was a barmaid partial to pulling more than pints of bitter. Even in pre-DNA days she might have got away with her indiscretions, but when Hubby pitched up to the maternity ward to see the new addition to the family, instead of being a blue-eyed, blond-haired Anglo Saxon, the poor little mite lay there with a full head of black wiry hair, half a Barbadian suntan, and a cricket bat. The old boy went ape-shit and had to be restrained from beating seven bells of shit out of wifey.

He went home that night, packed his bag, took the overnight train to Liverpool, signed onto the pool, and was last seen on a tramp ship bound for the Caribbean. One is left to assume he went there to try and balance the account.

All credit to the old girl, she took Sweep home, washed him, clothed him, and showered the child with love and affection. He grew up to be a tough, happy boy, and at fifteen joined the Army and ended up in the Parachute Regiment. Nobody fucked with Sweep. If the parachute insignia tattooed on his right shoulder was not warning sign enough, you only had to look at Sweep's facial features. There was considerable scar tissue around the eyes, and the Army had tattooed his blood group on his chest, so it was anybody's guess where he had plied his trade.

Sweep was never reminiscent about his Army days, but the rumour mill had it he spent time in Northern Ireland and was up to all sorts of skulduggery. There was supposed to have been a scene in some squalid bar down some squalid back street, where Sweep was unwinding after a job with a couple of the crew, and in rolled a bunch of rednecks. As the alcohol took over, the rednecks were becoming more and more objectionable, with one in particular picking on the weakest member of his own crew.

Nobody took any notice when Sweep got up to use the toilet and followed the redneck. When he got back, he quietly suggested they all leave. And everyone knew that when Sweep said to leave, you left. The last they heard of the redneck, he was in hospital having his face put back into shape.

Sweep had been the inter-services boxing champion at his weight, and there was a procession of boxing managers wanting to sign him up when he finished his service time. But he had no thoughts in that direction. He had dedicated nine years to the Army, and that was all the dedication used up in one go.

From a company perspective, they were only too happy to sign on ex-Army boys, as they knew they could drop them in some shithole where oil comes up and they would not be whimpering to return home before a week was out.

Sweep was possibly the most popular of all the hands that Fudge had to work with – hard working and loyal to the point of obsession. As for George, it was anyone's guess.

Fudge hurriedly telephoned Rebecca but got the answer phone. "I'm off to Egypt, possibly six maybe seven weeks," he explained. "Take care of yourself. Fudge."

As Fudge was making his way down to the company bus, which would have to do the rounds and pick up the crew, Newey's parting shot was, "Get the fucking job done, get the service ticket signed, and if in the 'Comments' section there's a tick in the VG box, you can overnight in Amsterdam on the way home."

Fudge knew that was both a blessing and a nightmare. A blessing in as much it gave the crew something to look forward to; a nightmare because Fudge would have to dig out his crew from various all-night bars or cat houses.

"Get something straight. Anybody comes in here after the fucking job with a sick note, saying they've got Tulip disease or some other fucking exotic disease that they've picked up off some old Tabbie, don't think you're getting time off or paid."

The final stop was the King George. Lush, after years and years of heavy drinking, looked in half presentable shape to board a plane, but for Nonce, it looked very doubtful. British Airways had had some incidences of oilfield hands getting tanked up coming home from Saudi, so now had a policy of not letting people on planes if they were intoxicated.

Fudge had a couple of hours at the airport before booking in, so all he could do was try to at least make Nonce coherent. As Nonce was bundled into the minibus along with his kitbag, Tony the driver took one look at him and said , "That fuck's feet won't touch the ground if he barfs up in this bus and I've got to clean it up."

"All right, Tony, just get us to Heathrow," Sweep came back.

The journey toward Heathrow went to plan until the bus hit a series of roundabouts. The swaying in the vehicle was too much for Nonce and he cried out, "I'm going to be sick. I'm going to be sick."

Tony stopped the bus in an instant, much to the indignation of the following traffic. "Get that fuck off my bus!" he yelled.

The door slid back and Nonce stumbled out. He managed to walk across the pavement and support himself against a shop window, arms outstretched, crucifix fashion. Sadly, the shop window belonged to a pizza restaurant. Fudge looked up, and life seemed to take on the appearance of a slow-motion movie.

Sitting in the restaurant was a very well-dressed man and a lady (his secretary or some other mystery). Nonce looked at the couple through glazed eyes, and they looked back at him in disgust. Then all of a sudden, Nonce released a shower of regurgitated matter that splattered the window and then started to run down.

"For fuck's sake, get that prick into the cab and let's get the fuck out of here. I know the arsehole that owns that restaurant, and I'm going to have a sawn-off shotgun stuck up my Jacksie and the trigger pulled!" cried Tony.

Nonce was bundled into the minibus, and Tony hit the throttle in blind panic. Fudge looked out the back window to see a waiter remonstrating with clenched fists at the departing vehicle.

Such is life.

Fudge turned to Lush and asked, "What's this George like?"

Lush, always the man of many words, said, "There's not much of him; all prick and ribs from what I could see."

Fortunately, when they got to check-in Fudge recognized the lady at the counter. This lady must have seen thousands of people a month, yet she remembered Fudge. Maybe it was the fact that he passed through so many times, but whatever the reason she gave Fudge a look and indicated that if Nonce did not get through at the boarding gate it was not of her making. Somehow Nonce did make it onto the plane, and needless to say, Lush was at the sauce immediately the wheels left the runway.

The Bear

The job went well, the crew did get a tick in the VG column, and Newey was good to his word and arranged an overnight stop in Amsterdam. The crew were staying in a popular hotel used by all the service companies supplying men to run the oil industry. All scrubbed-up and clean-shaven, the boys were in the bar at seven o'clock to start a marathon drinking session.

Fudge did not want to be a killjoy but had half his mind on home and Rebecca, so he told himself that he would have a couple of jars with the boys then have an early night. That all went out of the window, though, as also in the bar that night was Bear. He and Fudge went back a long, long way.

Bear stood six foot six, with a huge mane and beard, and his hands were enormous. Bear was a fitting name, for there was no mistaking he was a bear of a man.

Bear had his gang of boys with him – all Texas, Oklahoma and Louisianna. It was High Noon in the bar, for Fudge and Bear had had a few run-ins together. If push had come to shove, Bear would have prevailed, but he knew he would be licking a few wounds after any encounter. And as with all bullies, they don't like getting hurt.

But tonight, Bear had started drinking early, and it was the drink that was about to do the talking.

"Bear, fancy seeing you here," was Fudge's opening shot.

"Don't give me that bullshit," came back Bear. "I haven't forgotten that little stunt you pulled on me in Bangkok."

"But, Bear, how was I to know it had a pair of nuts?"

"You goddamn knew that was a transvestite!"

Sniggers started to come from his own party but were abruptly halted when Bear snapped his head around and bared his teeth at his gang.

"Seriously, Bear, do you really think I'd set you up like that?"

"Yeah, I think you would, arsehole."

"Look, Bear, I think you better take it easy with the Jack Daniels."

"Fuck you," growled Bear. "I heard you were in town, and I want a piece of your arse."

"Look, Bear, we've just finished a shit job and we're on our way home. We just want a quiet drink. What will it be?" Fudge offered.

"Shove it. If I want a drink, I'll get my own." It became apparent Bear was in a pissed-up state and was looking for trouble.

"OK, Bear, I've tried to be decent about this." Fudge could see Sweep was preparing himself; in his world, he who got in first usually came out the best. Fudge gave him a look as if to say "Steady". "You're obviously very upset about something, so how about we have a little competition? And just to make it interesting, you lot empty your pockets and put your dollars on the counter, and we will do the same and cover it with pounds. Winner takes all."

"I'll have some of that,' said Bear, and he gestured to his crew to empty their pockets. Fudge's gang did likewise.

"What will it be, arsehole? Wrestling? Arm wrestling?" came back Bear.

"Spoons."

"Spoons? You're shitting me."

"If you don't want to play, Bear, that's fine by me." Fudge went to pick up his money but Bear's enormous hand grasped his wrist.

He turned to his boys and said, "If this arsehole pulls any stunts, holler." Then he let Fudge's wrist go.

"It won't be me you're going up against, Bear. It'll be George."

"What! This little shit!"

By this time, George was having apoplexy. His imploring eyes never left Fudge's face. He desperately wanted to be one of the boys but knew Bear could rip him apart.

"This *little shit*," Fudge replied, "has never been beaten at spoons. You're looking nervous, Bear."

Bear had painted himself into a corner, and he knew it. Backing out now was a no-no, but even in his Neanderthal brain he could see he was being set up. "You watch this arsehole's every move," he told his troops. "He blinks, you tell me."

Fudge had to smile. Bear's arsehole was twitching, and this gave him the advantage.

George, meanwhile, stood there shaking. Fudge whispered something conspiratorially into Sweep's ear, and he disappeared behind the bar and into the hotel kitchen. Two chairs had been arranged approximately four feet apart, facing inward towards each other.

Fudge was running the show, and this kept him in the ascendancy; Bear was taking the orders and being led to slaughter. Bear's gang had sided with their man and were assembled around the chair he was seated in, with a dessert spoon sticking out of his mouth. George was seated opposite Bear, again with a spoon extended from his mouth, and Fudge stood behind him, rubbing his shoulders in professional boxing style and whispering encouragement to the young man.

"OK, Bear, as you're the newcomer to spoons, we'll let you have first hit."

At the word 'hit', George went to get off the seat. But with Fudge's hands still rubbing his shoulders in a downward motion, he could not move.

"This little shit ain't looking too comfortable," Bear sneered and returned the spoon to his mouth.

Fudge knew poor George was at the point of collapse, so he kept proceedings moving and gesticulated to George to lean over in his chair.

"Right, Bear, the name of the game here is for you – with that there spoon sticking out of your considerable mouth – to whack Georgie Boy here over the back of his head. Just so we are keeping this fair, I'll give you a little tip. Grip hold of either side of the chair with your hands, as it gives greater momentum and power at the spoon on impact."

What's this, George was thinking to himself, *helping the enemy? Here I am bent over in a chair, miles from home, eyes squeezed shut, expecting a spoon to crash down on the back of my head, and my friend, my boss, my man is telling the opposition how to inflict the maximum amount of pain. What's going on?*

Before George could think any further of impending hospitalisation, Bear attempted his first hit. He thrust down with all his considerable power, but as the spoon made contact with George's head, the spoon flew from his mouth.

After the first sudden surge of pain, George was wondering what the real thing would be like if this was a mishit. He rose from his bent over position, and his eyes implored Fudge, *Please get me out of here.*

"Over you go, Bear, it's the champ's turn. If you want to throw the towel in now, that's fine by us and we will just mosey on out of here with the money and no hard feelings from our side."

Bear was trying desperately to see a way out and save face. He knew something was going down, but couldn't figure out what. All he could see in front of him was a scrawny kid sitting in a chair with a spoon sticking out of his mouth. Still giving orders for his gang to tell him of any shenanigans, Bear bent over. Meanwhile, Sweep had returned from his errand and had attached something to the back of Fudge's jeans.

"It's showtime, Georgie Boy, and we need a first round knockout," encouraged Fudge.

George was about to make his first attempt, but Fudge pulled him up short and, with his right hand, removed the implement Sweep had attached. It was a soup ladle. One of Bear's gang was about to protest, but Sweep gripped him by the arm and motioned for him to keep stum. At heart, even though their man was going to be on the receiving end, they also considered him an arsehole so they each looked at each other and said nothing.

Fudge held the ladle in his right hand and aimed at Bear's napper. The head of the ladle did not move far. It was reminiscent of Tiger Woods approaching the 18th green at St Andrews. With just a hundred yards to the pin and just a break of the wrist, maximum power was despatched from club head to ball, only in this case it was Bear's head and the club was a ladle. A thud could be heard on impact and everybody winced. Bear did not move.

He sat bent over for what seemed an extreme amount of time then raised his huge hands to his head, and as he rose from the bent position, he pulled his head through his hands and came up to the sitting position. Seething through clenched teeth, Bear looked at all and sundry for an explanation, but none was given.

Round Two began, and it was pretty much a repeat of Round One, except that Bear's technique had improved, and the pain inflicted to George rose accordingly.

The look on Bear's face, though, said it all. *What the fuck is going on, and how do I get out of this?* was running through his mind.

Over went Bear. He sat, his eyes darting from side to side in the vain hope he would see something untoward and have the excuse he needed to call a halt. This time around, Fudge made no attempt to be discreet with the ladle, and he indicated to his gang to be ready to move. Instead of aiming the ladle on the top of Bear's head, he waved the implement in front of Bear's eyes as he was bent over.

Things did not register initially, but after a few moments, with a sudden rush it dawned on Bear what was on the way. Before he could sit up, though, Fudge had his neck in a vice-like grip. And with a swing of the ladle, it came crashing down on the top of his head, and Bear collapsed in a heap on the floor.

George, still sitting, had no idea what was going down when Fudge grabbed him by his collar, and in the same motion picked up all the money and ran, his gang following suit. When Bear finally rose to his feet he began jumping up and down on the spot, arms flailing everywhere, Jo Cocker-style, and could be heard down the street shouting, "He's dead! He's dead! He's fucking dead!"

Fudge and his boys were by this time safely ensconced in the Banana Bar. Monies from the Spoons escapade were duly dispensed over the bar, and the drinking began. Banana Bar had a speciality – one of their show girls would pace up and down the bar totally naked. Her claim to fame was she could lower herself and pick up paper money with a certain part of her anatomy, and that did not mean her hands.

George, starting to feel the effects of heavy drinking, was manhandled horizontally onto the bar. Fudge took a ten Euro note, folded length-wise in half, and laid it across George's nose. The show girl straddled herself across George and commenced lowering herself.

He didn't feel a thing as the money was removed from George's face, and the showgirl walked away with the note between the highest part of her legs.

George rose from the counter with a beaming smile. Sadly for him, he was starting to look bad, but give him his due he hung in there. By this time, the bar was just about packed with locals, tourists, and oilfield trash. It was time for George, unbeknown to him, to perform "The Dance of the Flaming Arsehole". With trousers and shirt duly dispatched, he found himself naked on the bar, music pounding in his head, a rolled-up newspaper protruding from the cheeks of his backside which had, for effect, been set on fire. As the paper burned down, George's movements became more erratic until the flames were lapping his rear end, and the smell of singed hair permeated the air. As if on cue, a round of beer was thrown at his lower half and the flames put out.

By this time, George was a blubbering wreck. But the show went on.

On stage, a chair had been positioned in the centre, and one of the show girls was sitting naked, legs astride it. A ramp had been positioned several feet away, on top of which a man stood, butt naked, wearing only a pair of roller skates. With crashing music, the man rolled down the ramp and coupled with the show girl, simulating a sex act.

Jeers arose from the Fudge camp. The MC appeared on stage and, as with all Dutch people, spoke impeccable English. "I see we have some oilfield boys in tonight. Perhaps one of them could give us a better show."

Fudge looked at Sweep, Sweep looked at Lush, Lush looked at the Captain, nobody looked at Nonce, and George looked out of it. In unison, the cry went up, "Georgie, Georgie, Georgie." George looked at Fudge, and Fudge wanted to help him. But in this game, weakness was seized upon and exploited.

"At some time we've all had to do it," was about all Fudge could manage.

So, Georgie Boy stood, still in his birthday suit, naked but for a pair of roller skates on his feet. The show girl had taken her place on the chair, centre stage. With music now just short of rupturing ear drums, tourists, locals, oilfield trash, and bar staff were all busting to get a view as George descended the ramp. Approaching the showgirl at speed, George could not fathom out what was happening, because the showgirl was not there. She had deftly got up and removed the chair.

With an imploring look at the crowd, George whistled past where he should have been coupled with the showgirl. The MC had by this time gone to the back door at the rear of the stage, and in a gesture of "This way, sir" George – still full speed – found himself bollock naked but for a pair of roller skates in Canal Strasse. The crowd in the bar went hysterical, the people in the street sniggered, and George wanted to cry.

That night, Bear had vented his spleen on some poor unsuspecting soul in some seedy bar in the worst quarter of town. He returned to his lodgings in the early hours and found pinned to the door his American dollars and a caricature picture of him with a huge red bump rising from the top of his head and a flaccid penis protruding from his forehead. That said it all: "Dickhead".

Next morning was a sorry sight, and Fudge had to rally his troops. Somehow George had managed to survive, but he was now lying in bed, his head to one side, while a huge plume of vomit lay on the blanket. Pop stars had died that way, but George was to fight and roll down a ramp another day.

Coming Home

Flights away from home base are usually a subdued affair, and the flight back home – although it should be a time of celebration – can be quiet. This flight home was no different, with the exception of Lush, who was keeping the stewardess busy with top-ups. The rest of the crew looked out of it.

George looked as if he was on borrowed time. Fudge guessed when the young lad got home, the telephone would be taken off the hook, curtains would be drawn, and that would be it for seventy-two hours. Nonce would no doubt be in the office first thing in the morning, giving his distorted version of the events of the last five weeks.

Fudge couldn't give a shit. His mind was on only one subject: Rebecca. He had had more than enough relationships, but in nearly all the cases it had been purely lust on both sides. This, though, was different. Although the friendship was at an early stage, Fudge did not want to spoil things by coming on too strong. Yet with time being so precious, because there was so much work pending and the next location could be a seven- to eight-week job, he felt he had to make the moves.

He knew Rebecca had had her romances and dalliances; it would be naïve of him to think otherwise. A lady in her position, with her lifestyle and schedule, must continually have to diplomatically fend off the offers. So, Fudge pondered the best way to entertain a lady like her. He already knew clubs were a bore to her, restaurants would be nothing new, theatre and cinema would hold no interest. He resigned himself to tackle the problem as and when it occurred.

Picking up his baggage and clearing customs was always a traumatic affair. Whether it was Fudge's appearance he could not tell, but for some reason he was nearly aways picked out for a customs search. He remembered on one occasion when things had nearly got out of hand with a customs official. He had just finished a gruelling job in Thailand, and when he got back to Heathrow, again he was singled out. The customs official totally emptied Fudge's bag, including his wash bag, and he even took the music cassettes out of their cases. Everything was left strewn across the counter.

As the official walked away, Fudge asked very politely, "Would you kindly put it back the way you found the bag?"

The official replied, "Who me?"

"Yes, you."

"Who do you think you are talking to?"

"You," Fudge remained calm as he went on, "I would Iike you to put it back the way you found it." By this time, a number of passengers had stopped to see what was going on, but the official totally ignored him.

After many journeys through British airports, Fudge was aware that customs officials carry no identification, no numbers on their epaulettes, so in effect are answerable to no-one. Again, still being very polite, Fudge asked, "Would you get your supervisor out here?"

The official still totally ignored Fudge.

By this time, there was a build-up of passengers all wanting to see this stand-off. At that moment, another official appeared. This man had no uniform as such, and Fudge guessed this was the top banana. Looking at Fudge, he said in a very aggressive voice, "You, come with me."

Fudge followed this man into a small room. Standing no more than five feet two, he turned to Fudge with a finger outstretched and growled, "Let's get something understood here. I can make life harder for you than you can ever make it for me. Now, I suggest you pack your bag and fuck off."

Still very polite, Fudge asked, "What's that mean? Something going to be dropped into my bag, a little bit of Bob Hope or something else?"

The official by now was beside himself. "You see it anyway you like."

As Fudge was about to leave the room to go pack his bags, his parting shot was, "You know, there are people out there that can help. That short man's complex of yours can be sorted out." Back at the counter, he packed his bag then looked across to the first official. "You pathetic little man," Fudge told him. "Take that uniform off and you're nothing. One day we just might meet this side of the counter."

The official was over in an instant. 'You threatening me?"

Fudge replied, "You see it anyway you like" and walked off.

This time, there were no hold-ups and his bag was quickly cleared, then Fudge took the underground into London. One of his highlights about coming home was Victoria Station. Long haul flights are mostly overnight flights and arrive very early in the morning at Heathrow. After clearing customs and taking the underground, Fudge usually found himself sitting on the forecourt at Victoria Station, with a newspaper and coffee in hand, just watching the hordes of people streaming off the trains on their way to work. Fudge had all the time in the world.

This time around, Fudge made his way to the pay phone. Dialling Rebecca's number, he was fully expecting to reach the answer phone, but it was clear from her "Hello" that he had wakened her from a deep sleep.

"Jesus, I was expecting you to be away somewhere," he said, immediately feeling guilty.

"Got back from New York last night, had to close down some paperwork, then did not get to bed much before three," came the sleepy reply.

"I'm sorry to have woken you," he told her. "I'll call a bit later."

"No, no, that's OK. I need to get up and start moving. So, how did your trip go?"

"Uneventful, usual stuff. Can I see you in town for lunch?" he asked hopefully.

"That would be nice. How about we meet in The Market Porter, say about one-ish?"

Fudge grinned, feeling pleased with himself and the world. "Look forward to it," he told her. "Bye."

Later that morning, Fudge took the train into town. Not only would Fudge be drinking, but he knew it was a hopeless exercise driving into town with all the midday traffic. He assumed he would be there first, as Rebecca's 'one-ish' seemed to suggest she would possibly be late. But to his surprise, she was already there and had managed to get a table in the busy pub, and was sitting with a bottle of wine and two glasses.

Fudge leant over and kissed her on the forehead.

"Took the liberty of ordering for you," she told him. "They do the best steak and kidney pie in town. Trust that's fine with you?"

"Fine," was Fudge's reply.

The meal, the wine, the company were all just fine. Again, time ran away, and Rebecca eventually said that she had to get back to the office. Before she left, Fudge asked if he could see her that night.

"I'd would really like that, but we have some clients in town, and I have to take them to a show tonight and then to supper, you understand," she said. "I'll call asap and we will meet'."

Fudge said his goodbyes and made his way back to the station and home. A doubt did briefly cross his mind: clients? Paranoia had never been a part of Fudge's makeup, but he couldn't somehow avoid the thought.

First day home for Fudge was always a subdued affair, what with all the travelling. So, after a short power nap on the settee, he made his way down to his local for a couple of scoops with the boys and a game of hunt the lady. Later that evening, he made his way back home, switched on the TV, and watched the last part of the ten o'clock news with the football results. Not being particularly partial to Northern teams, he was none too happy to see the top dog up there winning again. Ablutions and bed were the order of the night.

Fudge was in a deep sound sleep when the telephone rang.

"I said I would ring asap," Rebecca began.

"What time is it?"

"One thirty. I'm feeling pretty pleased with myself as I just took a big order. I have to do the paperwork and get the legal team on it in the morning, so I said to myself, if I'm awake, why shouldn't you be?"

"You want some company?" he offered.

"That would be nice, Fudge. By the time you get here, I will be all but done."

Fudge was showered and driving toward town as the BBC 2am news came on the car radio. On arrival, he went through the same procedure to gain entry, and once inside he found the door to Rebecca's apartment ajar. He entered with a soft knock.

"Come, sit down, pour yourself a glass. I'm very nearly finished." Rebecca was sitting at a table very close to the window which offered a stunning view of the Thames down to Tower Bridge. The shimmering river, with the reflected street and building lights, was a beautiful sight synonymous with only London.

Rebecca had her reading glasses on, her hair bunched up and held by a turtle shell clip, and she was simply dressed in a tracksuit. Fudge did not disturb her, as he could see she was totally engrossed in her work. The background music was courtesy of Gretzky.

Fudge had never been a serious music buff, probably because he had been put off it at his secondary school. The music teacher there had suffered the misfortune of having to take Class LC8 to Wigmore Hall for an afternoon recital. No doubt the composer had spent five years of his life putting his piece together, only for it to be panned and ridiculed in St. Petersburg, or Vienna, or Berlin perhaps, and as a tormented genius had cut off his left leg or some other part of his anatomy and followed this by drinking a bottle of Domestos or the equivalent tipple of the day – all before his twenty-fifth birthday. And now it was being played in front of five hundred South London scallywags from various schools, whose academic prowess left a lot to be desired. The man was entitled to top himself.

All hell was breaking loose amongst the children, who were totally out of their depth. Fudge had a flashback of that man on the violin, scraping away, the sounds of which were excruciating.

Fudge took a seat on Rebecca's settee and lifted a magazine off the Rimu table. Expecting *Country Life* or *Tatler* or *Horse and Hound*, Fudge was surprised to find it was a football magazine. Thumbing through the publication, Fudge became aware Rebecca had finished her work and was sitting watching him.

"You go to matches?" she asked.

"Arsenal is my team," he confirmed. "Don't get much time to get there, but I still follow them on the radio when I'm overseas. What's your interest?"

"My boss has a director's box at the Gunners."

Fudge sighed. "Lucky man."

Rebecca came over and sat on the same settee, and again Fudge was confronted with that look, that silence. Finally, she spoke. "Come here, Fudge, and kiss me."

Only too happy to oblige, Fudge initially made his move then checked himself. This was a different kind of girl, different set of circumstances. Here was a lady in her prime, intelligent, successful, witty, everything in life to play for. He asked himself, *What am I doing here?*

It seemed as though Rebecca was reading his mind. "You look a little nervous."

"I am, Rebecca. I sure don't mind and I'm certainly not complaining, but I'm asking myself what I am doing here," he replied honestly. "I'm a bit of rough. Are you pretending to be walking on the wild side and I'm the uncut diamond before you meet and marry the merchant banker or the CEO?"

"That's your call, Fudge," she responded. "Why don't you let it all play out the way fate has decided?"

Fudge got up, took Rebecca by the hand, and led her to her bedroom. Undressed and in bed, with just the lighting from the forecourt outside, Fudge and Rebecca entwined. And their love making was extreme. Extreme in as much as this was not just some easy knock-off, another to have a laugh about with his mates down the pub. It swung between being passionate to being brutal, caring to almost sadistic; they soothed each other, and they were vicious to each other. This was an encounter Fudge would never forget and would never share with anyone, not even his mates down the pub.

Both were startled by the alarm clock; it was 7am. Rebecca got out of bed. "Stay there, I'll make coffee," she told him.

Fudge, due to work habits, was up when Rebecca had finished with the bathroom. Sitting at the table overlooking the Thames, they sipped their coffee.

"Hope you enjoyed the show last night," he said.

"Don't be crude, Fudge. I could see it was something special."

"I'll give you a call in work today, if that's alright?"

She nodded. "That will be fine."

Fudge knew that a lady as dedicated to her work as Rebecca would need space and time to prepare herself for the day. So, he said his goodbyes, gave her a kiss, and left.

When he got home, it wasn't even nine o'clock, and already there were three messages on the answer phone. Fudge smiled to himself, wondering if Rebecca was giving him a wind up. That thought, though, was abruptly changed on hearing the first message. It was Newey in a panic.

"There's been a major fuck-up in Holland. All hell has been let loose. Call the minute you get in!" The next call was ten minutes later, again Newey.

"Where the fuck are you?"

The next call, again Newey. "You better not be holding out on me, sitting there letting your answer phone take the calls."

Just as the third message finished playing, the telephone rang again. Fudge knew it would be Newey.

"Get down to Gatwick, humi humi over to Amsterdam, and get yourself a taxi out to Pernis," he was instructed. "Shergar has let the fucking tanks overflow. If it's gone over the bund wall and the skimmer tank, we all can say goodnight and will all be looking for a job. Before you say it, I know you have just got back, but this is serious. You know the people over there. Sort it out, take them out for dinner, anything. Just don't lose that contract."

Fudge sighed. "Newey, you know Shergar is a nightmare. I've bailed his arse so many times, but he gets all the easy numbers because he fucks everything up. I'm really pissed about this."

"This is the oil business, Fudge. You've been around long enough to know you are married to it. Just do your best and do what's got to be done to sort the mess out in Pernis. And stay in touch." With that, Newey was gone.

Fudge immediately called Rebecca on her mobile to explain; she was in her office.

"Pity, I just arranged to get you into our box for Arsenal's home game on Saturday, but no worries," she told him. "Someone else will be only too happy."

When Fudge put the phone down, he knew Rebecca was not greatly excited about his going away.

Pernis was not a mess; it was a disaster. Shergar, who was supposed to be on nightshift, was either watching porn or, as Fudge suspected, fast asleep after being on the piss all day. And he had let the tanks overflow. There was thick, heavy viscous crude oil everywhere. Fortunately for everyone, it had stayed within the bund wall, which was what it was designed to do. However, the skimmer tank was full to overflowing and would have to be vacuum trucked out.

Adjacent to the lease was a dairy farm with cows by the hundreds. If crude had got in there, compensation would have gone through the roof. Fortunately, Fudge was on good terms with the major running Pernis and had a good track record with them. Peter Keipers just gave him a look of 'We've been here before'.

Fudge shrugged his shoulders. "Shit happens."

Keipers had the courtesy to pull Fudge to one side. Unlike most oilfield people, he took no delight in humiliating someone.

"Your man will have to go," he said in no uncertain terms.

Fudge nodded. "I understand, Peter. I'll get onto it right away."

"I think we have to count ourselves very lucky," Peter explained. "This could have turned into a serious incident. I'll get with our people and start a clean-up. You better tell your Mr Newey that I hope his insurance policies are up-to-date, as this is not going to be cheap."

Fudge went to the site office and relayed the messages to his boss. There was a brief silence, and Fudge wondered if Newey had passed out on the floor. Seconds later, he came back.

"Get that arsehole Shergar home. He's finished. He's let us down one too many times."

Fudge wondered if Newey had imparted this piece of news hoping he would tell Shergar and Newey would not have to. But he knew that wasn't his boss's style; Newey would get great delight in bulleting Shergar.

As for Shergar himself, Fudge found him in the hotel bar – where else? The man had gained his nickname from the horse teeth he carried in his mouth, but Fudge thought him a sad figure. Everything Shergar touched, Shergar fucked up – mainly due to the piss. His marriages, his working life, his private life, it was all a terrible mess. Nevertheless, he was a cunning bastard; a survivor. He had put three men in hospital in Tunisia due to an error – another occasion when Fudge had been forced to bail him out.

"Well, Shergar, this is another fine mess you've got me into," Fudge told him.

But Shergar was beyond caring. He knew he was on his way out. No doubt he would get another job somewhere else till they discovered what a liability he was, then he'd move on again. It was a damning indictment of the industry.

"You can tell Newey his operation is crap," he snapped back.

"I suggest you do that yourself, Mark." It was the first time in a long time Fudge had called him by his name.

Fudge went off to call Rebecca. "Looks like a three- or four-day clean-up," he explained.

Rebecca suggested, "I've got to be in Antwerp this Thursday and Friday. Why can't we meet for the weekend?"

"I'll have some of that," replied Fudge. "How about we meet up in Bruges?"

"I'll have some of that," joked Rebecca.

Several days later, Fudge and Rebecca met up and booked into a quiet pension on one of the many canals that Bruges boasts. For Fudge, the city was one of Europe's best kept secrets. A city steeped in history, with museums, canals, wonderful cafes serving coffee as it should be served – not like the cats' piss served up at home – and of course the most beautiful beer in the world. Occasionally the city's football club would play against a British team in some European competition or other, with the resulting hooliganism and mandatory clearing up afterwards.

Spending time like this with Rebecca, Fudge was aware of her intensity. Everything this lady did she did in full measure. Making do was certainly not in Rebecca's make-up; mañana would not be tolerated.

Reading was one of her passions, which suited Fudge. Although not a prolific reader himself, he was a person who liked to think things through. Never one to rush headlong into situations, he preferred to take a step back, assess, then make his moves.

Now, several moves were afoot for Fudge, and he really needed a career change. He knew he was one of Newey's boys and that the boss genuinely liked him, but Fudge knew in his heart of hearts he would still be sorting somebody's shit out if he stayed. He also needed to move home permanently.

Being single, he had been in a position to accumulate a decent amount of money working overseas, where everything was provided and basically you kept everything you earned. But now something had come into Fudge's life, and a whole different agenda could be on the cards. That something was Rebecca.

Hours passed by, with Rebecca engrossed in her book and Fudge enjoying his beer and taking in the local colour. Walking the canals and peering into churches, museums, and buildings that were the birthplace of some famous merchant, painter, or writer, gave the pair of them ravenous appetites. Again, the lovemaking was intense and unforgettable.

Whether he liked or not, knew it or not, Fudge was falling in love. If anybody had said it to him, he would have said they were talking crap, but there was no doubt about it, he was going down fast. Was this the end of a legend? Had Rebecca done what countless other girls had failed to do – made him feel content, comfortable with himself, and at the same time manage to bring him out, introducing him to a slightly different world, one definitely more cultured than the one of his past. He had been subtly introduced to classical music, although not the deep heavy type, a different genre of film, and he would never have thought he would have enjoyed a night at the opera – albeit not too deep. Rebecca knew his limitations and only pushed it so far.

When Fudge and Rebecca returned to London, life took on some kind of pattern. Fudge still had his Friday night out with the boys, usually ending up in his favourite club close to home. Saturdays he met up with

Rebecca, but no matter what time they returned home, Rebecca was always up early Sunday morning and went off to her parents' London home in Golders Green.

Religion was a subject that had never been discussed between the two of them, but Fudge did wonder if the Friday and Sunday family gatherings had some religious connotations. He and his brother Jo had been borne to relatively old parents, and with the family history of cancer striking both sides of the family, they had both been barely adults when they'd had to fend for themselves.

Fudge was not envious of Rebecca's close knit family structure, but he was just not privy to it. Again, he was aware that very soon he would be called away again. He knew the next few days would disappear in the blink of an eye, and time spent overseas would be a terrible grind. The routine of oilfield work, on top of which the location was invariably run by an arsehole, meant the six to seven weeks away seemed like six to seven months.

Return to Saudi

Fudge had handed his passport into the office to get a Saudi visa processed, so that took the guessing out of where his next location would be. It was several years since Fudge had worked there, but it had been his very first location and he had some fond memories of the place. The young, raw recruits were all eager to get on with the job, to impress, and hopefully to get a better handle on life. He wondered where several of his former colleagues might be now. After a few years with the service company, some joined the major oil companies and went into management. But this had never been an option for Fudge.

The thought of taking work home every night and just the four weeks holiday per year were enough to curb any inclination in that direction. If your face did not fit, or you were not greasing the right man higher up, you could end up in some hell hole. Some of the men that did have a modicum of talent, but could not grease, had the misfortune to find themselves in these places. There were the supposed benefits in management – firstly, field work was over and done with, and of course there was the pension – but there were countless dissatisfied and disillusioned men in oilfield management. Possibly, he decided, this was why they were all such disagreeable fucks.

One thing was for sure, the oil industry did not give a man a dollar without taking the equivalent of two in return. The countless wars since the commercial discoveries of the early nineteen hundreds, right up to the present days, had claimed lives in the tens of millions and would possibly continue until a viable alternative was found.

The inevitable telephone call from Newey came, and Fudge was told to be in the office early morning then down to Heathrow and away. Fudge noted he was flying solo, so he presumed he would be replacing someone who had either done his time, told the company man to "fuck off", or was going off horizontal in a stretcher.

The flight down to Dharan was the usual morbid affair, packed full of oilfield men having to leave home to maintain the supposed good life. Fudge thought of the alternatives. He knew he could never compete financially with the Fishers. He and Rebecca had an enviable lifestyle, but at what cost? The failure rate of relationships in the oilfield was extreme; if not the highest, then it was very close to it.

He had seen seriously hard men reduced to nothing because wifey thought a bit of extracurricular activity would not go amiss to brighten up her mundane life. Your partner had to be very understanding or very ambitious. Fudge had heard so many times the story of "I'll only be in this game for a couple of years then I'm out". But the oil game was insidious, creeping up on you, and before you knew it you had committed yourself to the big house, the big boys' toys, the flamboyant lifestyle – and then you'd be up to your neck in debt.

On arriving in Dhahran, the first thing Fudge noted was the new terminal that had been built. On his first journey down, the modest terminal had just a couple of conveyor belts that serviced the incoming planes. The stench created by the oppressive heat was overpowering. Here now stood a palace; massive chandeliers with works of art hanging, all enclosed in a structure made of solid marble, and all maintained to an agreeable temperature by massive air coolers hidden from the eye. Not a breeze block in sight.

The airport was named and dedicated to the ruling family of the kingdom, and they were letting it be known in no uncertain terms: "We are not just rich, not even obscenely rich; we are rich to the point where we can affect the world's economies, and don't you forget that."

The company vehicle and driver were on hand to pick Fudge up and whisk him to the office or guesthouse. It turned out to be straight to the guesthouse, which Fudge was informed was in a security-gated compound, and it was company policy that once you stepped out of the compound you were effectively on your own.

Fudge was shocked at the change in Dhahran. It had transformed itself from a one-horse town into a huge metropolis. Hamburger restaurants were everywhere, shopping malls in abundance. Gone were the days when you went down a dirt track and into the gold souk to do deals or buy your bootleg CDs from a street vendor. The new buildings were designed to service the American Forces who had set up shop with their huge military bases.

Fudge was not happy seeing the huge security presence that surrounded the compound. It covered a huge area with tennis courts and a swimming pool, which Fudge was told were for management employees and their families only. *So here we are, all in the same boat together, and still there's a fucking pecking order*, he thought.

Fudge wanted to ask, "Should we get overrun by insurgents, does the pecking order work in reverse, i.e. the dross are beheaded first, and management reserves the right to be the last people standing?"

From being in a land that had once been friendly, warm to foreign people, people who would open their houses and their lives to you, he was now standing in a fortress to keep those same people out. What a tragedy. Where had it all gone wrong?

Fudge was to spend three days at the camp, waiting for the site documentation to be processed. He unpacked, showered, and made his way down for the evening meal. The eating arrangements were structured so that permanent staff, if they wished to eat out, were allocated a meal time and the plebs stampeded the place an hour later. Fortunately for Fudge, there were two menus. One was catering for the large American presence and comprised of obscenely large hamburgers, chicken wings and legs, which no self-respecting swan in Hyde Park would look out of place wearing, and soft drinks and coffee by the gallon. The alternative, which was more to Fudge's liking, was structured to non-Americans. That is, it did not have hormones, colour, cholesterol, or additives by the sack load.

Unfortunately, Fudge was the only non-American on the camp, but this did not stop him from joining some of the Americans at the meal table. He was staggered at the conversation, and diplomacy the order of the day. He was in no doubt in his own mind that the coalition forces were there for one reason and one reason only – oil and self-serving interests, and to maintain a regime that was dependent on outside help to maintain that flow of oil.

To Fudge, on hearing these boys telling him "that America was sick and tired of being the world's policeman, and somebody else created this mess and those same people should have to clear it up", it just did not add up. He wanted to ask, "Who's feeding you this crap?" but thought better of it. These boys genuinely believed there was no hidden agenda; perhaps they were right and Fudge had it all wrong. Perhaps these boys, whose vice president was formerly the president of the very company that they were now employed by, that very same company which had been on the floor prior to hostilities but had soon made a miraculous recovery on the stock market.

Fudge amused himself exercising around the camp, listening to his music, and doing plenty of sleeping. Finally, the day came when he loaded his kit into the company four-wheel drive and made for the desert. After six agonizing hours driving over that rough terrain, the drilling rig finally came into sight. Pulling up outside the company man's office, Fudge went inside to introduce himself and was immediately hit by the freezing cold that the air conditioners were pumping out. It was obvious by the man's weight and stature that the chair he was sitting in was about as far as this man travelled in a day.

Introductions over, it was time to get his kit unpacked, change into coveralls, and make for the site and equipment he would be working with for the next six to seven weeks. In his early days working in the desert, the vast majority of the drilling crew would be Brits. This went with the service companies that supplied men and equipment to maintain and keep functioning all the various operations necessary to drill a hole, flow the hydrocarbons, and assess the potential. That's before even thinking of pipelines, production plants, shipping, refineries, and finally the tank of your car.

Those days were gone. With the exception of the company man, tool pusher, and a couple of service hands, the entire crew was made up of cheap labour – Indians, Far Eastern men, and Eastern Bloc. Gone were the days of friendly banter in the Mess room, talk of football, who was screwing who, the occasional porn movie.

The work was punishing, but the pay was good, and days rolled by. But Fudge instinctively knew this was going to be a nightmare of a trip. If your equipment, as was usually the case, was not maintained properly, you could be out in the searing sun trying to get a pressure test for hours and hours. In the companies' pursuit of profit, they had trimmed every conceivable cost imaginable – labour, spares, maintenance. Even the food was crap, as too many catering companies were undercutting each other to get a contract, and this was reflected by what was on the plate.

The days of profit were gone. In today's world, profit was not enough; there had to be obscene amounts of money rolling into the company accounts to satisfy the accountants and the directors, who smugly watched the share price rise, knowing they were in for their windfall allotment of shares at the end of the year.

What concerned Fudge more than anything else was the safety aspect. He could not blame these men who come from grinding, distressing poverty, taking work for what to Fudge was a pittance; the money was beyond anything they could earn in Mumbai, Bangalore, or wherever. For Fudge, seven weeks was his cut-off point, but these men would stay out for months on end. The men back in their air-conditioned towers could not give a tuppenny toss about the boys in the field.

Fudge had had a lucky escape on an earlier job, when an Indian crane driver has lifted a load instead of, as requested, lowering it, and he had crushed Fudge's hand in the process. Fudge had resigned himself to having a disfigured hand for the rest of his life, but the gods shone on him that day. He was shipped into hospital where he was fortunate enough to have an exceptionally gifted Egyptian surgeon rebuild his hand. After he was sent home, Fudge thought that as the accident was not of his making, he should be entitled to some form of compensation.

He went to a solicitor who formally wrote to the company's head office in Paris. Fudge was immediately sent a plane ticket and told to be in the office next day. When he got there, the company solicitors and assorted big wigs were in attendance, and Fudge was given his marching orders for having the effrontery to ask for compensation.

On returning home, Fudge met up again with his solicitor, who told him, "The accident happened in the Middle East, it was an Indian crane driver, you work for a French/American company which is worth several billion dollars, and you want to take them on. Where do I start? I think you just have to count yourself lucky you still have a hand."

Lucky was certainly the operative word. Fudge knew of a pleasant, hard working Nigerian boy who'd had the misfortune of being in the wrong place at the wrong time. He was cut in half by an underrated coupling which had been installed and blew out, as it could not take the excessive pressure that had been applied to it. So much for company loyalty – the days of decency were long gone. Let's all bow to the money god; long may he shine over us.

In the early days, if there was work to be done in the base, there was a golden rule that it did not matter how blootered you got the night before, it did not matter how much of your time you spent in a cat house, you always turned up for work on time the next day. Fudge recollected a French base supervisor who went by this rule. He liked a drink himself and he was good to his men if they did their work. He did his best to get men out on time for their field break and did everything he could rather than call them back early, but that was now a distant memory.

The days dragged on and on. Due to the remoteness of the location, Fudge could not get to a town to make a call to Rebecca. And there was no point in asking the company man. That would cost money, and we don't want to piss the money god off, do we?

Finally, the day came when Fudge packed up his gear, boarded the company four-wheel drive, and made for the city. Then it was on to the airport. The flight back to London was a raucous affair and the stewards were kept up all night plying the boys with alcohol.

Once again, Fudge found himself on Victoria Station forecourt in the early hours of the morning, watching the crowds disembarking from the trains. This time around, Fudge decided he would wait till he got home before making any calls.

His first call was Rebecca's home, where he left a message on the answer phone to say he was back. A call to her office informed him that Rebecca was in New York for possibly another two days. Fudge wondered briefly if he should buy himself a cheap return flight but thought better of it. Rebecca would almost certainly be up to her neck with dealing and entertaining, and the last thing she would need was Fudge in tow. The time waiting for Rebecca to return home could be put to good use.

First day back invariably meant a trip to the office to hand in service tickets, expenses, and post job reports. This always led Fudge into conflict with Newey. As a typical company man, Newey always tried to save a buck here, trim a buck there. Fudge could live with that, but what he hated was writing out appraisals. In a business where cliques were prevalent and the North/South rivalry unhealthy, he had been the recipient of damning appraisals to his personality, attitude, and ability. These reports no way bore any resemblance to the truth. It was simply a case of Fudge not kissing arse or telling a less than competent supervisor that he was "the greatest thing since sliced bread, and how did the oil industry ever function before you graced us with your presence?".

Newey knew Fudge could not tolerate arselicks, but it was company procedure and he had to go along with it. After the mandatory office visit, Fudge would invariably return home and wade through the mountain of mail that had accumulated in his absence. Getting bills paid before the threats to have him cut off from the essentials of living were a priority. Next came a visit to the supermarket to stock up on goodies, and the last port of call would be the pub.

Fudge spent the next day touring around the myriad of estate agents that abound in the desirable prosperous parts of town, and he was staggered at what little you got for the excessive amounts of money required. He hoped Rebecca would be home for the weekend and maybe have some time off, as he'd like to spend some time down in Bexhill and Rye. They were parts of the coastline that seriously appealed to Fudge, and he was mulling over moving out to either of them to get away from the hectic life that was London.

Two days passed and there was no word from Rebecca. This started to concern Fudge, as Rebecca would normally be in constant touch with the London office by telephone and email, and they would have given her a list of calls she had received in her absence. Fudge never liked to pressure people, simply because he disliked it coming his way, but he did ask himself on several occasions if he should call again. He felt sure she was not the kind of girl to leave him on a piece of string, and if she wanted out she would tell him one-on-one.

Late on his third day home, he received the call he had been waiting for. Rebecca sounded exhausted. She asked Fudge about his trip, but as the conversation continued, he was aware of a distance that had come between them. Fudge felt he should address this and ask if her work was getting on top of her and whether she needed more time and space.

"More time, more space? That's the problem, Fudge," she told him. "There's far too much time and space between us. I understand you have your work, but I'm finding it difficult never knowing where you might be tomorrow. I don't even know if you are safe. What kind of relationship is that?"

"At least I can take a positive out of this, you care about me," he said, smiling to himself.

"Care about you? There's hardly a night goes by when I don't think about you, get concerned when I hear on the news that oilmen have been held hostage somewhere, or that an aeroplane has gone down that services an oil company in some remote location. It's no life, Fudge. Fortunately, my work keeps me busy and takes away the pain and distress."

Fudge had no answers, and they both hung there on the telephone, neither speaking.

Eventually, he managed, "We have to meet, Rebecca. I've just had seven weeks of hell. Let's at least try to sort this out."

Rebecca said she would be home late that night but would wait up for Fudge to come by at midnight. He arrived with a bottle of their favourite wine and a small gold pendant he had bought in the gold souk.

"It's beautiful, Fudge," she told him.

"Guess it's not as grand as some of your gifts of the past," he replied.

"Why do you keep referring to my other life, Fudge?" She frowned in frustration. "You keep selling yourself short and you hide your light under a bushel. You're as good, if not better, than many a man out there. Please just for once forget about your past and don't remind me of mine. I'm sure it will make life better for both of us."

Fudge took Rebecca in his arms, and they kissed, looking at each other briefly before making their way to her bedroom.

"Not a good time to have returned home," she apologised. "The painters are in. Guess that's what's making me a bit edgy, but it's still nice having you here beside me."

"I've been sharing a room with three other men for God knows how long, so this is Paradise for me," he told her. And, lying beside each other, they both drifted off into a deep sleep.

Probably still jetlagged or possibly just savouring the moment, Fudge did not wake up till very nearly ten o'clock. Rebecca was engrossed in paperwork.

When he emerged from the bedroom, she told him, "You can turn right round and go back to bed and I'll bring coffee."

Turning on the television in the bedroom, Fudge caught up with the last of the news. It was all pretty much the usual stuff until an article came on about some editor of a newspaper who had printed some controversial sketches which had aroused and antagonised Muslims. This man was saying he was justified putting this to print. Fudge, though, was seething.

He knew this man wanted to be controversial, and his move would no doubt sell papers, but Fudge knew that alienating Muslims directly or indirectly put his – and all personnel working particularly in the oil industry – in peril. Rebecca had been standing in the doorway, two mugs of coffee in hand, and was listening to the segment.

Fudge turned to her. "What an arsehole! There's men out there with families just about to get on an aeroplane for Saudi, and this turd is coming out with this crap. It's plain unfair on their families. Something should be done. The government love nicking your money in taxes but do nothing. What is it? Oh yes, freedom of speech. I know about your history, Rebecca, but this editor would not dare to do a similar article ridiculing the Jewish faith; it's more than his job would be worth."

Rebecca did not speak but simply handed Fudge his coffee then undressed and lay down beside him.

After several minutes, she turned to him. "You're getting very bitter, and that's not you, Fudge. You really do have some serious decisions to make – us, your future, your whole life. I'm really not happy with the direction we are going in."

Fudge took her mug from her hand and turned to face her.

"Let's not go down that avenue for now. I just want to enjoy every minute while I can," he told her.

Newey informed Fudge of the lull in activity, but Fudge knew it was only going to last so long. In the oil game, you were either working flat out or you could go weeks on end with nothing. For a lot of men, it was always a cause for concern. Whilst the base salaries were good, they really made their money when they were on ticket. A lot of men were so committed with debt that in some cases they needed twenty-five days a month on ticket just to break even.

Of course, this gave the companies the edge. How could you tell a Newey to "wedge it", knowing the banks, mortgage companies, car loan operations, and credit card companies would be hanging you out to dry if you failed to pay on time. It always amazed Fudge that men could allow themselves to be in such a compromising situation. Fudge had always had a mindset that if he couldn't afford something, he didn't want it.

Consequently, the committed men would be hounding Newey every day to get them out during the slack periods. But this suited Fudge. He was all too aware that the day might come when he had a family and all the pressures that went with it, but until that day came around he had his time and his space.

The rumour mill had it that there was a contract coming up in Thailand. Fudge gave himself a smile; he knew full well the manoeuvring and arse licking that would be going on behind the scenes to get on that one. Fudge had done a couple of trips to Thailand, and he'd found it all quite tragic. He had seen men throw a twenty-year marriage and the kids out of the window because they had found paradise in a young attractive Thai girl. And in just about every case, it always ended in tears for these men. He remembered one case where a coworker of his, who Fudge considered a stable and committed man, fell for a girl twenty-five years his junior. Knowing he was walking on dangerous ground, Fudge had tried to make this man see sense.

"No, Fudge," the other guy had argued as they sat in a makeshift bar that had been set up just outside the camp perimeter, "you've got it all wrong. This really is love. I've met the family, and they're lovely people."

Fudge might have guessed he was batting on a sticky wicket; the sarong the guy was wearing said it all. There was no way back, at least for now. And sure enough, two years down the line, after this man had spent a bunch setting up the family in a beautiful home and financed a chicken farm, he was paid the family visit with the inevitable final scene: 'you leave vertical or horizontal; the choice is yours'.

"I should have listened to you, Fudge," the guy told him later, "but I guess I was blinded. My home situation was not up to much, and I really thought I'd found it. But if it's not the passport to UK that they're after, it's your money. Still, two years were memorable, and they can't take that away from me."

Two memorable years? Great, but now what did he have? Diddle squat, maintenance for the first family, and now living on memories in a bedsit. Sad bastard.

Another aspect of Thailand that did not appeal to Fudge was the party scene. Fudge liked a drink and was all too happy to have a look around and take in the local colour, but that was as far as it went. The thought of getting involved with hookers did not appeal to him. Thinking he could be the fifth one that day for that hooker was not exactly foreplay for him.

He recalled a young recruit, who was probably just like George, getting laid by a girl from one of the many bars in downtown Bangkok. When the guy got back home, he started to break out in a rash and discharging, so he went down to the VD clinic. They did whatever VD clinics do and sent him home. Two hours later, there was a police car outside his parents' home to pick him up and take him back to the clinic. Apparently the clinic were in a panic that he might start spreading this particular strain of VD into the community. By all accounts, the doctor told this boy that he had a real cracker of a dose.

"Never seen the likes of it before," the doctor told him. "We think there might be a couple of medicines that might kick it, but no guarantees. If they don't work, I suggest you might have to go back to Bangkok, as they might have more knowledge on this particular strain."

No guarantees! And all for a Donald Duck! He was probably pissed out of his brains at the time and got mugged into the bargain, and now he was carrying this shit lying dormant for the rest of his life, only for one day for it to wake up and make his life a misery again.

There was an even sadder case again in Thailand where Fudge had been working a land location, again with the mandatory bar erected on the perimeter fence. He was having a beer with an Aussie boy who told Fudge that he was on borrowed time. He had picked up a strain, and there was no way back. Fudge was amazed at how sanguine this boy was.

"No good getting excited, just have to take one day at a time," he told Fudge. "I'm told it won't be too pleasant later down the line; affects the brain, by all accounts."

"Your folks must be devastated?"

"Haven't told them," the Aussie guy admitted. "Hopefully they are gone before I reach that stage, and they don't have to agonize."

Finale

The days with Rebecca went by all too quickly, and Fudge knew that soon the telephone would ring, he would have to pack his bags, say his goodbyes and leave. He noticed how Rebecca became exponentially quieter as the days passed.

"The family are having my sister and Terry over for Sunday dinner, along with some other people," she told him. "They would like us, and whatever is left of your family, to come."

"I have only a brother, and I really do not think he would go down well with your family," Fudge replied.

"You can't keep him squirreled away forever."

"You really would not like his politics. He's a person who was good to me when we were younger, but he's a radical," Fudge admitted. "He's not antisemitic; he just loves a fight – not in the physical sense of the word. Pitching up with a sprog and a girl out of wedlock won't go down a bundle either."

Fudge was wondering if this was a set-up. *Was the family trying to create barriers? Were they unhappy with their girl seeing a relatively unknown quantity? Mr Fisher struck Fudge as a man who was not a zealot – quite the reverse – but when it came to something that could be long-term with his girl, could it be a different story?*

And so the Sunday arrived, and Fudge picked up his brother from what passed as his home. "Trish's mother is sick, and her dad can't cope on his own, so she is spending the weekend with them," he told Fudge.

"Get something understood," Fudge replied. "I really like this girl. You know her background, and I would appreciate it if you would go easy with the politics."

His brother shrugged. "You can leave me here and just say I was not feeling too good, if that would make you feel better."

"Jo," Fudge sighed. "You're my brother. For better or worse, you will always be my brother. I think you fucked up in life, but that was your choice. All I'm asking is you show a little diplomacy."

"Enough said."

After picking up Rebecca, the trio made their way to Golders Green where the Fishers' magnificent house stood in a private park.

Jo turned to his brother. "Nice little two up, two down."

Fudge hoped this wasn't a sign of things to come.

Terry offered Fudge his hand, and Fudge instinctively knew Terry was going to savour the next couple of hours. Fudge was then introduced to Mr. Golgenfeld – a top city barrister, who probably represented the Fishers in one way or another. Terry's betrothed looked stunning.

Aunt Estelle made her way over, and Fudge introduced his brother. Jo, when it suited him, could be utterly charming and polite, and Fudge was breathing a little easier that Jo just might be in one of his subdued moods. The party were seated, and formalities began. *Was the waiter service a full-time thing in this household, along with the catering?* Fudge wondered. *Or were they bought in for the occasion?* Either way, the food and wine were superb.

Fisher turned to Fudge. "Been home for a long spell this time. Are you due out soon?"

Fudge explained the vagaries of the oil industry and how his side of the operations worked, trying to put a shine on what was basically a shit job that didn't pay badly. Golgenfeld entered the conversation and asked Fudge what his thoughts were regarding the long-term stability of the oil industry.

What Fudge wanted to reply was, 'Why ask me? I'm just a fucking monkey out in the wilderness who swings a hammer, knocks up pipe, puts a whole load of data down on paper for some whiz kid in town to decipher and tell the grossly overpaid slobs upstairs whether the hole they have just spent a hundred million dollars on is viable or not.'

Instead, he cleared his throat and waded in with what he hoped made some kind of sense. Relief for Fudge came when the conversation was taken over by Rebecca and her sister, and their sibling rivalry was quickly apparent. Digestifs were served, but Fudge politely refused, saying that he was driving and felt better not going over the top with alcohol.

"Nice to see a young man being responsible," commented Aunt Estelle.

God, that one must have irked Terry, Fudge reckoned. A sudden thought entered his mind. *That bastard Terry had set this all up, this little jolly-up was of his making.* He could envisage Terry the previous Sunday, saying, 'Why don't you invite Rebecca, Fudge, and his family over for Sunday dinner?' already knowing that Golgenfeld would be in attendance.

He already had the inside track on Jo, so would Golgenfeld go to work on him? Would this be a fifteen-rounder going to the wire? So far Jo had remained silent, but that was all about to change.

Terry chirped up, "Jo, we have not heard much from you. Care to tell us about your family, your work?"

"Not really much to tell you, Terry," Jo replied. "I live with a lady in South East London, and we have a daughter. As for work, I do a little private teaching."

"Any particular field?"

Yeah, the field I'd like to get you in and punch your fucking lights out, you arrogant successful turd, Fudge thought.

"I usually help out kids struggling with their mathematics," Jo explained.

"You should come up to our accounts department. I'm convinced there are some people there that need a little help in that department," offered Mr Fisher, and polite laughter went around the table.

Not letting Jo off the hook, Terry asked about his schooling. When Jo name-dropped the highly regarded grammar school he attended, Golgenfeld asked if he knew "that political animal Nevis" who taught there.'

Joe nodded. "I had many a run-in with Nevis."

"How so?" asked Golgenfeld.

Jo looked up at his brother, and both knew the interrogation had begun. *Should they bail out now while they were in front or stay and become chopped liver?* the look suggested.

Fudge could have possibly halted proceedings there and then with an excuse that he had to be home, expecting a call from overseas regarding work or some other perfunctory excuse. But he asked himself how long he could keep running and hiding his brother. Sooner or later Jo was going to have his say; better to get it over with now.

"Nevis should never have been allowed to teach," Jo told Golgenfeld. "He might be Oxbridge but that does not give him the divine right to expound his distorted view of the world on vulnerable pupils. He was a champagne socialist. I often wondered if he was homosexual and wanted to have run with Philby and his gang of thugs."

"You do not think much of Philby? I do not think most pupils at that time would have even heard the name," Golgenfeld replied.

"What I think of Philby as a person is immaterial, but as far as I can see he was the lowest from of life – a thief. He stole people's wives, their reputations, their lives. He knew he was part of the Old Boy network and knew he would be tipped off when it got too hot. That man was responsible for the deaths of thousands of people who were not in it for the game." Jo was in full flow now. "If he were to have ever thought they would throw him in the central heating boiler, like they did Penkovsky, he would never have had the balls to play espionage."

The conversation was lost on half the company, including Fudge. For all he knew, Philby could have been the left back for Millwall Football Club.

'And your thoughts on the situation on the Middle East?" asked Golgenfeld.

Jo looked at him directly before replying, "I'm a guest in this house, and I think I should conduct myself accordingly."

The lawyer scoffed. "Oh, I think we are all adult people here, and a debate on what is now affecting every man in the street will not be amiss."

"Please," Jo sighed, "I'm asking you not to ask me of my thoughts in that direction."

Like a bloodhound, Golgenfeld would not let the matter drop, though. Decades of experience on the bench were kicking in, and he was luring Jo into committing himself. Jo knew it, Fudge knew it, and that supercilious turd Terry knew it. He was savouring every moment of Fudge's discomfort.

Fudge resigned himself to the inevitable. Either this family would be horrified, or they would take it in their stride and think that Jo was a misguided, disillusioned, angry young man who had spunked away his life, his intelligence, and any possibility of a stable and dignified life.

"Please tell us your thoughts," probed Golgenfeld.

Jo looked at Fudge, but this time it was not a look for help.

"You're your own man, Jo," his brother told him, "and if these people really want to know how you feel, then maybe you should tell them."

"The Middle East is a tragedy," Jo began. "The Arabs have become the whipping boys for Israel. There are Arabs who have a legitimate right to live in certain quarters of supposedly shared territories, but they are being stopped at checkpoints and made to wait hours and hours before being allowed to go to their homes. I watched a television programme where a British journalist carried a hidden camera. It showed Arab children being stoned by Israeli children while Israeli guards stood by and did nothing; where a huge brick wall was built not three feet from Arab houses, supposedly for security reasons; where Israelis get unlimited water, but the Arabs live on a gallon a day and one hour of electricity. The Israelis want them out, and they are making it a war of attrition.

"The Israelis are taking away the Arab culture, their spirit, their soul," Jo went on. "And it's plainly unfair. The constant reminding of the Holocaust and the persecution has to stop. If this was happening anywhere else in the world, it would be called ethnic cleansing. There are a million-and-a-quarter Arabs who have a legitimate right living in Israel, and the Israelis want them out.

"I have to sit and watch Israeli foreign ministers spinning their way around justifying slaughtering innocent children. They are so eaten up with greed and animosity, they are sick. I do find it amazing that every time there are elections in Israel, hostilities seem to come to the fore, and any potential leader has to show how tough he or she can be. I would not be surprised if they were not initially putting up the rockets themselves to get hostilities going. After all, Israel has a very healthy defence business, and there's nothing like trying it out on the real thing.

"You cannot hold the world to ransom for something that did not happen in most people's lifetime. I understand that a madman took away millions of your people and that must never happen again, but six hundred thousand Rwandans were hacked to death in a week, Pol Pot is said to have murdered two million people, Stalin, Idi Amin, Bukasa, the list goes on. But where are their Kristallnachts, their museums. We are all aware the Jewish people have the American presidency in their pocket, but we are paying too high a price to satisfy one particular nation." Golgenfeld continued prodding. "The Israelis have a right to those lands," he said.

"On that premise, give Australia back to the Aborigines, America back to the Red Indians," Jo told him. "Come to that, give England back to the English. I cannot see it happening, can you?"

"And where does your own country stand on this?"

"Where does Britain stand? I watched a documentary made by an Australian journalist who went to Iraq and documented the plight of Iraqi mothers watching their babies die for the want of a fifty pence injection. I sat and cried as I watched the programme. There was supposedly an embargo in place on Iraq that denied these people medicines. OK, you're eighteen and carrying a Kalashnikov and you're a threat, so shoot them. But a baby?" Jo shook his head. "God, I do not know how our Prime Minister and his obsequious wife can live with themselves. I'm convinced it's only their arrogance that gets them through. If I had my way, they would be standing in The Hague to answer questions on crimes against humanity."

The silence around the table was deafening.

"So, what do you consider to be the answers?" Golgenfeld continued.

"There are no answers, Mr Golgenfeld, we've gone beyond that. I really think there is no turning the clock back. For what it's worth, if there is light at the end of the tunnel, I think the Israelis have to sit down and talk – seriously talk. But not go through the motions, then a day later bomb a beach and kill women and children, then follow that up by destroying a neighbouring country, or taking out somebody they don't like or consider a threat without a trial."

Golgenfeld frowned. "That's a little extreme."

"Ask Dr. Bull if it's a little extreme."

"That man was prepared to take out a nation," Golgenfeld replied.

"He still never had a trial. What other country could do such a thing, take out whoever they like, settle old scores, take out peace activists that they consider an irritant? They are a nation above the law, simply because they are answerable to nobody, and this makes them dangerous in the extreme. It's in Israelis interest to talk, and the reason I say that is because a day will come – certainly not in my lifetime but possibly in my child's time – where an Arab boy or girl who has seen their home destroyed or their parents run over by an Israeli tank, just might grow up to be very capable in nuclear physics and design a device that could devastate the Middle East. This device would not have to be delivered with an F14; it will arrive in a Thermos flask. A sobering thought, don't you think?"

"It would sound as if there is a conspiracy against the whole Arab world?"

"Mr. Golgenfeld, I really may have this all wrong and the coalition are there purely for reasons that I am not aware of," Jo conceded. "But to me, when a country has a four hundred billion a year defence budget, you have to justify this to the American public who directly and indirectly are paying for it. You justify it by saying that you are fighting a war on terror. To be able to fight a war on terror, the first thing you have to do is create terror. Again, I may be reading the facts all back to front, but have the Americans not been in over one hundred incursions since the Second World War, and it's all been purely to keep the world free? When you take a man whose only gift is opportunism, and an adulterous one at that, and somehow aspires to become the leader of our country, and as a thank you for your country's involvement in conflict, he somehow becomes a substantial stockholder in the third biggest defence manufacturer in the US, I personally find that repugnant.

"How do you think a mother or father must feel who has lost a son or daughter in conflict, and for what?"

Fudge felt sure his brother would know there were no arguments being offered up from what was effectively the other side. This was no debate.

Had Terry gone through a similar initiation? he wondered. Fudge knew Terry would kiss a turd in the pursuit of advancement and would have been subservient, sympathising and almost apologetic. But whatever his tactics, he had passed the test.

Golgenfeld continued, "Do you think this country should pull out of the coalition?"

"Our PM loves the attention; he craves the limelight; he wants to be a world player. He was hoping he could do in the Middle East what Thatcher did in the Falklands, i.e. fight a war and win, and then be remembered and go down in history as one of the Greats of Britain. He seriously thought it was going to be a walk in the park." Jo was back on his soapbox again. "I was fascinated at watching an interview with a Presidential adviser whose history went back to JFK, and he said publicly that when the forces went back into Iraq, they thought it would be done and dusted in three months. Then it was to be the turn of Syria, which again would be a three-month sojourn, and then into Iran. In nine months they thought they could take over the Middle East.

"Sadly, it's all gone terribly wrong, and what has he left us? A country living in fear. His legacy will be spin. There's no doubt he is one of the most accomplished politicians ever, but if you take away the rhetoric, people are terrified to get on a bus or the underground. The terrorists only have to put out a rumour and the country goes into a panic. His predecessor was an incompetent adulterous sleazeball, and before that it was nepotism.

"We are now fighting a war against a foe that will become more and more formidable. These are not a bunch of thugs that are total losers, belligerent, angry, lost to society, the result of a massive underclass that has been allowed to breed in this country. These are highly intelligent and educated young men and women, dedicated to a cause – however misguided – and more than prepared to lay down their lives. How can you defeat or even compromise with somebody who is prepared to make the ultimate sacrifice?"

Golgenfeld nodded. "It is certainly not a picture of happiness, but surely you must offer your child hope?"

"I fear that history will repeat itself, and sadly she will have to live through another world conflict before people see sense," Jo told him.

Thankfully for Fudge, the conversation began to alter course. But he knew that when he left with his brother, the family would dissect everything that had been discussed.

Rebecca's demeanour had changed, and when dinner had finished she said that she would be staying over with her family, so Fudge drove back to South London with his brother. Conversation between them was limited; both had their own ideas of how the afternoon had gone and were mulling it over.

Finally, arriving at Jo's squat, Fudge turned to him. "I'll stay in touch."

"You do that, Fudge." Driving home, Fudge knew there would be resentment toward his brother. If he had lost half his family to a nutter, he would have been resentful, but of course Fudge had never known conflict or seen a war as such.

He returned to his apartment, switched on the radio, then noticed the answer phone had a message. He instinctively knew it would be Rebecca.

Sitting on his settee, he let it play. "Fudge, I love you dearly, and I will always have a place in my heart for you, but this cannot go on. In another life, another time, we could have made it work. Please don't call me, and don't tell me you want to run away with me to Brazil. That shit only works in Hollywood. I have family, we have a history; it will only bring us into conflict. I wish you well, Fudge, and I sincerely hope you find happiness. You're a good man and no-one can take that away from you. Goodbye ,Fudge." The phone went dead.

Fudge could feel the raw emotion in her voice. It was final; there was no going back.

He let the tape play again while John Lennon was giving it his best from the radio. *"Here I stand. head in hand, turn my back to the wall, now she's gone I can't go on, feeling two feet tall. Hey, you've got to hide your love away."*

Thank You

www.ingramcontent.com/pod-product-compliance
Lightning Source LLC
Chambersburg PA
CBHW030237180626
46810CB00008B/3179